Lynda La Plante was born in Liverpool in 1946. She trained for the stage at RADA, and work with the National Theatre and the RSC led to a career as a television actress. She turned to writing – and made her breakthrough with the phenomenally successful TV series *Widows*. Her two subsequent novels, *The Legacy* and *Bella Mafia*, were both international best-sellers and her original script for the much-acclaimed *Prime Suspect* won a BAFTA award, the British Broadcasting and Press Drama award and the Chicago film Golden Plaque award. Lynda La Plante was also awarded the Contribution to the Media award by Women in Film. Her latest novel, *Entwined*, has just been published.

LYNDA LA PLANTE

SEEKERS

PAN BOOKS
LONDON, SYDNEY AND AUCKLAND

First published 1993 by Pan Books

a division of Pan Macmillan Publishers Limited
Cavaye Place London SW10 9PG
and Basingstoke

Associated companies throughout the world

ISBN 0 330 33267 8

1 3 5 7 9 8 6 4 2

A CIP catalogue record for this book is available from
the British Library.

Phototypeset by Intype, London
Printed by Cox & Wyman Limited, Reading, Berkshire

With many thanks to Sara Lawson

CHAPTER ONE

Stella Hazard totted up the day's takings at the Bake O Bread, and noted that four chocolate éclairs were missing from the tray, but as she had slipped a nutty brown malt loaf into her own shopping bag, she couldn't really take young Maureen to task. She would, however, mention it when she came to work on Friday.

Stella worked part time, three days a week. The pay was minimal, but it all helped, and the company of the other women she worked alongside gave her a bit of a boost. Maureen was a plump, slow-witted girl who did the baking and more often than not ate her way through whatever was left over – especially anything with fresh cream inside or on top. She was not one for conversation, but Beryl, who worked full time at the Bake O Bread, more than made up for Maureen's monosyllabic mutterings. Beryl never stopped talking, from the moment she took her coat off in the morning until she left – as she had done today – early. As soon as the manageress had gone Beryl was on the move, with a couple of sliced white and any rolls she could lay her hands on.

'You don't mind, do you, Stell? Only I got the kids to get sorted, and I've not got me Hoover fixed. You'll be all right, will you?'

Stella, good-natured as ever, pushed the pink Bake O Bread cap further up on her forehead. 'You go, I'll clean up and see you Friday.'

Beryl, already heading for the back door, called over her shoulder, 'Yeah, see you, tarra . . .' Then, as she passed the bacon slices, Stella saw her whip a few rashers into her bag. Beryl was fast, faster at filling up her shopping bag than she was at serving. She had three children, all at school, but no

1

husband. He, according to rumour, had run off with a local barmaid. Stella had been tipped off by the manageress not to bring up the subject as Beryl could launch herself into a real tirade – and no amount of customers waiting to be served could stop the flow of her blow-by-blow account of the 'waster' who had ditched her for the blonde tart who had pretended to be a family friend.

Stella finished the takings, cleaned the counter, washed down the shelves, and then took off her overall and cap. Checking the time, she saw that it was after five fifteen. She grabbed her coat, changed her shoes, then put in a call to Mike's office. She hated the answer machine, it always made her feel nervous; she either started talking before the bleep, or waited so long that the bleep signalling the end of message time cut her off. She waited, knowing by now that if it rang four times the machine would start. Sure enough, the familiar voice began.

'You have called Seekers Investigation Agency. There is no one available right now. Please leave your name, number, and the time you called, and your call will be returned. Thank you. Please speak after the tone . . . B-L-E-E-P.'

Stella hesitated, and then spoke quickly. 'It's me, Mike. It's Stella, just wondered . . . er . . . well . . . nothing urgent, but give me a ring.'

On the way home Stella bought a chicken, a few vegetables and a bag of potatoes. She caught the bus and sat with the groceries on her knee. It was only four stops, then she had a short walk to the small terraced house in Henley Road. It was just starting to rain so she hurried down the road, lifting the latch of the gate, muttering to herself that she must get Mike to fix it as it always needed her to bang it open with her hip. She stood on the front step as she searched for her keys, the rain really coming down now, and she fumbled at the lock. She checked the keys. She'd only just got used to the new lock they'd had fitted when they moved in. Like the gate, the front door was stiff from the new coat of paint. She and Mike had

2

moved to Richmond seven months ago, but it still felt strange, and she didn't really know anyone in the street. The young couple next door left early and returned late, and on the other side there was a surly-faced woman who had seemed loath to utter even 'good morning' – although her cat used Stella's back garden as its toilet.

The hall was freshly painted, as was most of the house – the kind of fast decoration job done for a quick sale. Stella wanted to redecorate completely at some time, but had concentrated on the kitchen first. She placed her groceries on the pine table, then took off her coat. She returned to the hall, half expecting to see Mike's coat on the hook, but there was only his old mackintosh. She looked at her reflection in the mirror. The damp had made her blonde hair too curly, and she ran her fingers through the sides, then fluffed up the top. She sighed. She would start a diet this week. She could see the buttons on her blouse straining, so she pulled her cardigan closer. There was no point dressing up to work in the Bake O Bread; sometimes the whole place was like an oven, and the eleven o'clock rush for take-away coffee and sandwiches meant she was run off her feet. She had a quick sniff at her armpits, then headed up the stairs. It was after six now, so she had a bath, got dressed, and gave her hair a good brush before she returned to the kitchen.

The chicken duly stuffed, with a few strips of bacon over the top to keep it nice and juicy, Stella proceeded to peel the potatoes and put the beans in water. Opening the cutlery drawer, she took out two sets of knives and forks, found two glasses in the cupboard, and wondered if she should make a rice pudding or not. She turned on the radio, began to top and tail the green beans, then checked the calendar, a month-by-month 'Views of the English Countryside'. She counted the days. Mike was often away, a few days most weeks, but he always called in to say when to expect him home. It had been more than a few days, it had been . . . almost a week, and not one call.

Stella telephoned the office again: the same answer machine message. This time she was a bit ratty as she asked Mike to return her call. She was cooking a chicken, could he at least tell her where he was?

The lounge was immaculate, not a cushion out of place. Stella poured a sherry and sat on the sofa, watching the end of the news. She patted the cushion back into place before she returned to the kitchen to check on the chicken.

Stella ate alone, her eyes constantly straying to the calendar. Had she forgotten something? Had he said what day he would be back? Mike's empty place opposite hers made her unable to finish her dinner. She tried to recall exactly what he had said the last time she had seen him. He had been sitting where his place setting was now, wiping the residue of his eggs and bacon with some bread.

'Be gone a few days, Stell, same as usual, but I'll call you . . .' She had been washing the dishes, hating to leave a dirty kitchen, and had taken his cleared plate, cup and saucer to the sink. He had remained sitting, staring into space.

'Any mail?'

Stella had replied that there wasn't, and he had come and stood behind her as she dried his dish. 'I'll call you, OK?'

He was six feet three, a big, broad-shouldered man. Beside him she seemed tiny, and he had slipped his arms around her waist, kissing her neck. 'You do the best eggs and bacon, you know that?'

She had laughed, but before she could say anything he had walked out into the hall and run upstairs. He always washed his hands and cleaned his teeth after breakfast: it was a thing he had: he hated smelling of cooked food. He always used cologne, the same soft, soapy smell she bought from Boots every Christmas. In the small house she could hear him walking around above her and, on that last morning she had seen him, after making sure the kitchen was clean and tidy, she had followed him upstairs.

Mike was standing by the bedroom window, staring into the street below. 'You like this house, do you, Stell?'

'Yes, it's fine. I'd like to decorate it up a bit, but there's plenty of time for that.'

He had turned and smiled. Mike had a beautiful, slow,

4

boyish smile, head tilted to one side. 'You get whatever you need, I'll make a start as soon as I have some spare time.'

'When will that be, then?'

'Soon.' He looked at his reflection in the dressing-table mirror, adjusting his tie. 'I've got a big job on . . . be some good money, and then I can take a bit of a break.'

Stella remembered she had asked him then about the job, but as usual he had dismissed her question. He hated talking about business. She had enquired about the new office and again he had shrugged, saying that it needed a lot of work, but until he had the money it would just have to do. Then he had reached for her, drawn her to him and kissed her lightly. 'Be a good girl, eh! I'll call you in a couple of days.'

Mike had left, and she had picked up the jockey shorts tossed down by the bed. Then she had gathered up the towels he had left scattered on the bathroom floor, untidy as ever. She hunted around for socks and other clothes that would need washing. Stella hadn't worked that day, but washed, cleaned and ironed, then done some shopping.

She could think of no reason why Mike had not called, but not until she lay in bed that night did she begin to worry. He had left the Metropolitan Police almost eight months previously, and they had used the small legacy her father had left her to open up the Investigation Agency. It had all happened so fast – one moment they were living in Stoke Newington, the next they had moved to Richmond. Mike had suggested Richmond because he had found good premises for opening the agency. Stella had only seen it once, and she had not been quite as enamoured of the place as Mike.

The building was in an old, run-down boatyard, with an ageing wreck still left in the dock, a boat Mike had teased and joked about refitting for their retirement. He was good at spinning yarns, she had always known that, and when he said they would sail off together to retire to the Costa Brava, her imagination had run riot, and they had laughed together. When he had shown her round the office, his energy and enthusiasm had been infectious. She always kidded him that, even though she was the one from Dublin, he was the one she was sure had kissed the Blarney Stone . . .

The problem that had occurred was never mentioned: the fact that he had been forced to take early retirement with no pension. He refused to discuss it beyond saying that he had been 'framed', had been made a scapegoat. Stella had not wanted to press it further as he had been deeply depressed and shocked by what had happened to his career. One night he had virtually broken down, punching the wall with his fist. He had told her that he would prefer just to walk away, that it was impossible to fight the system.

Mike Hazard had been a police officer since he was nineteen years old. His anger and humiliation at the way he had been treated made Stella furious.

'I caught the gov'nor taking back-handers, Stella, but it all got twisted around. I'm not fighting the bastards, I wouldn't give them the satisfaction. I just walked out, told them to stuff their job. I don't need them, they're all bent. I want to make it, show them – I want to show them all. I'll start up my own business, I don't need them.'

In truth, Stella had been relieved. To begin with, Mike was at home more than he had ever been, and when they moved, it seemed like a new start to their life. She loved the house, but what she had not bargained for was how much work Mike had to put in at the agency to get it started. In fact, she had seen even less of him than when he had been on the force, but, he told her, it was only for a while, just until he could afford to get an assistant. Mike was confident the agency would take off. What *he* had not bargained for was the recession, so when Stella took the part time job at the Bake O Bread, the eighty pounds a week came in useful. The recession, Mike reckoned, would soon be over, and work had started to build. It was only a matter of time. At night he would lie next to Stella, describing what he was slowly getting together with the boat and the Costa Brava trip. He made her promise to stay away from the yard until he could show off his boat.

They had been married twenty years. There was a passion to their relationship. Not always lovey-dovey, they had their rows. Stella had quite a temper, Mike had a hell of one, but they loved each other. Mike was the only man with whom she had ever had a sexual relationship, and she could think of no other man ever taking his place. The only sadness in their marriage was that Stella had been unable to conceive. She had had three miscarriages and had been on fertility drugs for three years. The baby's room, the waiting cot – even, at one time, a pram she had bought because it was a bargain – remained covered in sheets, the door to the baby's room closed. The lost babies broke her heart, and he was there for her, comforting and understanding. Stella had been slender and, as Mike always said, the prettiest girl he had ever seen in his life. He watched as she put on weight with all the different drugs. He never complained, never joked about her plumpness, but was a strong, steady, loving husband. When Stella was told that it was doubtful she would ever conceive again as she had started the menopause early, Mike had sat her down and cupped her face in his hands. He told her that he didn't care about being a father, all he cared about was that Stella was fit and well. If she really wanted a child, then they would try to adopt. They had tried for a year, only to be told finally by the adoption agencies that Stella was too old . . . Mike had declared that he would take a trip up the Amazon and bring her back a baby after they had watched a television documentary. He could always joke her out of her depression. He was a joker . . .

Shortly after the failure of the hoped-for adoption, Stella's father had suffered a heart attack, and moved in with them so that Stella could take care of him. He stayed in the baby's bedroom. The pram and cot were given away. Stella had watched Mike carry out the cot. The young couple were delighted, the girl's belly swollen and her baby due in just a few weeks. Stella watched as Mike packed the cot into the boot of the couple's car. She saw him shake the young boy's hand, then gently touch the pregnant girl's belly. It was such a sweet gesture, it had made her weep – because she had known then just how much he, too, had wanted a child, a son . . .

Just thinking of it made Stella want to cry now. Her father

had died almost a year ago. After he'd come to live with her, she had washed and cleaned up after him, as he had become almost like a baby.

This new house was good: it had no sad memories and, like Mike had said, it represented a new start. Stella snatched a tissue from the box by her bedside. If they had known how much the old bugger had stashed away, they might have felt differently. Thirty thousand pounds. And all the years he'd lived with them he had never given them more than few quid from his pension. Stella blew her nose. Still. It had been a surprise, that thirty thousand, but it had enabled them to put down the deposit on the house and the office. Maybe if they'd known about it before, they would have spent it already. Possibly they'd have had a holiday – well, they would be going on one, in that boat . . . the Costa Brava!

Stella snuggled down under the duvet. She couldn't help but smile. Mike and that boat. She wondered if he would ever get it fixed up. Then she got to wondering again about where he was. It had been how many days?

Stella began to drift off to sleep, recounting the days Mike had been away, and yet, she was still not *too* worried. It was just odd that he had not called her.

Mike's place beside her in the big double bed was empty. His photograph on the bedside table, one that caught his boyish smile, was the last thing she saw as she fell asleep.

Susie could not get comfortable. She drew the pillow from the other side of the bed to rest beneath her stomach. It seemed that however she lay, her back still ached. She was hot, then she was cold, then she was thirsty, then she was hungry, and it was always for the same thing: peanut butter sandwiches. She had always hated peanut butter until this last month. Now it was all she could think of. 'I'm not getting up again!' she muttered to herself, looking at the bedside clock. It was after eleven.

The kitchen was littered with dirty crockery. She had meant to wash up the dishes, but felt too exhausted. Susie hunted through the fridge, the jar of peanut butter was almost empty. She unscrewed the lid and licked her fingers, then crossed to the bread bin. She fished around in the dirty sink and retrieved a knife she had used for her last peanut butter sandwich binge, and scraped inside the jar.

She sat down at the messy kitchen table which overflowed with books, newspapers and more dirty crockery. She told herself she must wash up, but that feeling of exhaustion swept over her again and she plodded back to the bedroom, slumping down. No sooner was she in bed than she was thirsty again. Bottles of lemonade and cans of orange juice stood at her bedside, and she proceeded to munch the sandwiches and drink from the lemonade bottle. The lemonade was flat, and she almost cried with frustration. She rubbed her huge stomach. 'I hate you! You know that?'

The baby kicked. Suddenly Susie was smiling, sensing each movement of the infant inside her. She wished Mike was here, she'd called him four times. He had promised he would come with her to the clinic, promised he'd help her get the pram. But he'd not returned a single call. She was getting really pissed off. Not only had she staggered out on her own and driven miles to pick up the pram, but she had also carried it up the stairs at home – in such a foul-tempered mood that she had banged it up each stair. Then she had called Mike's office and yelled, '*Where the hell are you?* I've got the pram, I had to drag it all the way back here myself! You promised you'd be here – where the bloody hell are you, Mike? Will you pick up the phone? Will you *call me!*'

Susie had made three further calls, each one more abusive than the last, until she had slammed the phone back so hard it almost cracked. She lay back, tucked the pillow under her back this time, then dragged Mike's pillow from his side of the bed to wedge it under her belly. She just got settled when she had to struggle to her feet and hurry to the toilet. The pressure on her kidneys and bladder meant she had to get up and down to the toilet three or four times a night. She was

9

exhausted and bad-tempered from lack of sleep.

The bathroom was a mess, washing spilling out of the plastic laundry bin. Susie splashed cold water over her face, then patted it dry with a grubby towel. She meant to do the washing, but everything seemed such an effort. She felt so bloated. She was – her ankles swollen, her breasts so heavy they made her feel like some kind of freak cow. The entire pregnancy had been a nightmare for her. She padded back to the bedroom, and the glimpse she caught of herself in the wardrobe mirror almost made her burst into tears: she was gross, she was like an elephant.

Mike said she was more beautiful than ever. He rubbed her belly with oil as she was worried about stretch marks. Her skin was a soft tawny brown. He had teased her, telling her that if the baby didn't have her deep brown eyes, then he wouldn't want it. Susie did have wondrous eyes: dark and vibrant. Her mother was African, her father – no one was sure who he was or what he had been as she had been adopted when she was an infant. Susie's adoptive parents had been elderly, and white. They had loved her dearly: she was a bright, eager child with a lively, quick mind. It was not until she began school that she encountered the racial taunts of other children; it was not until then that she even began to understand that she was different, she was black.

Susie enrolled as a cadet with the Met, and became one of the first recruits in her year to get promoted to plain clothes. She was good at her job. She loved the work, and her only sadness was that when she was moved to the fraud squad her parents were no longer alive. She met Mike a few years later. She had been living with another officer and was more interested in her career than marriage. She had never even contemplated having children. Her aim was to be Detective Inspector, and she was fully aware that she was being monitored, 'groomed' for moving up the ranks. Marriage and the imminent birth of the baby had put her career on hold. Not that she suspected Mike really wanted her to return to work. He'd never said that he didn't agree with it, but whenever she discussed the future, she just met a wall of silence . . .

It was difficult. She had left at the same time as Mike – loyalty to him, in some ways – but her superior had had a long talk with her, suggesting that she should think about returning. She did indeed think about it a lot, but she knew they would not be able to afford anyone to look after the baby – well, not until the agency was on its feet, and then maybe she would work alongside Mike. He wasn't averse to it, rather he had encouraged her, saying that business was looking up, and that perhaps by the time the baby was born they would be in a financial position to hire someone to care for it. He inferred that he had some big new client, but wouldn't elaborate as he said it was unlucky. When he knew more, he would tell her.

Susie sighed, pulling the pillow closer. He could make her so angry by being secretive, but maybe he was just being over protective. He was so caring about the forthcoming baby, checking Susie's weight, making sure she ate properly . . .

The agency – she had been into it once and was so disappointed. Mike had led her to believe that it was in a good location, but Susie thought that it was ridiculous to have an investigation agency stuck in a boatyard. Mike had become very tetchy, arguing that it was a good out-of-the-way place. Besides, private investigators were not like estate agents, they didn't wait for passing street trade but got their jobs by word of mouth. He had insisted that until he got the place 'ship-shape' – haw, haw – she was not to drop in. He was having it decorated, signs made, adverts and notepaper printed and so forth.

'What about that awful old wreck outside in the dock? That for clients, too? You planning on sailing up the Thames?'

Mike had laughed, his fabulous infectious laugh. The boat would be fixed up, and she would sail along the Thames out into the ocean . . . one day.

Susie looked at the clock, then eased her body round to open the bedside table drawer. She took out her diary. He had not called for . . . she counted the days. She was used to him going off on business often two or three days a week, but never this long without calling. Susie calculated it was almost seven or eight days since she'd seen him. She lay back, trying

11

to remember if he had said anything before he left. Had he mentioned something she had since forgotten? She could remember that he had promised to pick up the pram from the couple they had called. He had found the advert in the local Richmond paper himself, so that meant he must have been intending to be home that morning.

Susie yawned, half asleep. She was still not unduly worried, and she snuggled down, drawing the duvet closer. The last time she had seen him was when she was still drowsy and half asleep. He had sat by the bed, gently drawn back the covers and traced her face with his hand. 'How's my mama-to-be, then?'

'Fat,' Susie had muttered.

'Beautiful,' he had whispered, kissing her neck.

He always smelt so good, a soft, sweet, soapy smell. She had drawn him closer, wrapping her arms around him. 'I love you . . .' she murmured.

Mike had kissed her, then said that she should stay in bed, get as much rest as possible, and he would call. 'I'll be back in time for us to get the pram, then we should look for a cot, get everything ready for him.'

'What if it's a girl?' Susie had asked.

Already on his way out, Mike had turned at the door, giving her that lovely smile, the reason she had fallen in love with him. 'Well, you'll just have to start all over again, won't you?'

Susie had heard the front door slam, heard his footsteps on the concrete balcony outside the flat, knowing he would be turning towards the stairs down onto the next level. The flat was hideous but, like everything else, it was only temporary, until the business was on its feet. That was the last time Susie had seen him, and as she drifted off to sleep she counted the days again. It had to be eight. She wondered where the hell he was. Why hadn't he called?

The boatyard was in darkness, apart from a light in one window on the second floor of the old building. The blinds were half open, and the shaft of light cut across the cobbled yard and out onto the glistening canal, which reflected it like a mirror.

Mike Hazard stood with his back to the window. It was after eleven and he was beginning to get really pissed off. For the tenth time he checked his watch and half turned as he thought he heard the sound of a car. He waited, listening, but could hear only the lapping of the water as it drifted over the weir. He returned to counting the bundles of notes: twenty thousand pounds, fifties, twenties and tens. He stashed them in a leather holdall, zipped it up, and glanced yet again at his watch. He was over an hour late. Mike couldn't believe they could come this far and then the idiot foul up . . . He crossed over to his answer machine and flicked it on. Would there be a message?

The messages began replaying: Stella, Susie, Stella, Susie – 'Call me. Where are you? Call me.'

'Mike? Call me . . . Mike? Call me, it's Stella.'

'It's Susie . . .' He switched the machine off. Hearing the sound of footsteps echoing over the cobbles below, Mike switched off the office light. The bulky figure of James Donald halted in its tracks, his sweating face turned up to the unlit window.

'Mike? It's me. *Mike?*'

Kenny Graham checked his watch, then returned his gaze to the factory gates. Beside him, Tony Laytham sat cracking his knuckles, muttering, 'I told you that fat shit wouldn't turn up, he's gonna blow it for us. Where the hell is he?'

Kenny looked at the clock on the dashboard, then back again to the darkened factory. There were lights on in one section of the ground floor, more light from the security guard's office, but the rest of the massive building was in blackness.

Laytham turned to stare out of the back window. 'I'm not hanging around here much longer. It's a waste of time, I knew he'd run scared, he was shittin' in his pants last time I saw him.'

13

Kenny Graham lit a cigarette, snapping open the Zippo lighter. 'I can torch it. That way we'd know we'd be in the clear, that's my gig, I got everything I need in the boot of the car. What do you say?'

Laytham looked at his watch. 'We'll give him a few more minutes.'

Kenny snorted. 'Oh yeah? He's a bloody hour late, he's not gonna show! I told you – I said to you he'd foul up but you wouldn't listen. I didn't like it when he brought in Hazard, but you went along with that – you gone along with everything that fat shit wanted, now he's pissed on us. What if he and Hazard have decided to cut us out? They don't need us.'

Laytham lowered the car window. 'Bullshit! They need my dough, they wouldn't cut us out.'

Kenny shifted his weight and took yet another look at his watch. 'That geezer up at Ascot, he got dough. All we done is bring the bird to the cage. What's to stop them easing us out? And if it wasn't for me, none of you would have got to Donald. It was me. I found him.'

Laytham frowned, still staring at the dark factory. Kenny chucked his half-finished cigarette out of the window, staring at the lit end as it remained glowing in the darkness. 'I could get in, set a timer and we just piss off. If Donald comes, we just done the job for him – but with him not showing, it sucks. Unless he's with Hazard, and I don't trust that bastard. Ex cops are all shits, cops are all bastards. I don't trust Hazard.'

Laytham sighed. Kenny's prattle was getting to him, needling him, and again he turned to stare behind him to see if Donald was anywhere around.

'That batch of disks give 'em a direct lead to Donald, right? They'd suss out he was involved. I mean, that's what he was sent down for, right? We can't just friggin' sit here waiting for the fat bastard to show. I got twenty grand in this, you got twenty grand—'

Laytham flicked a half smack at Kenny to shut him up, then took a final look at his watch. 'OK, let's do it. Then we'll go round to his place.'

Kenny Graham's face lit up with delight, and Laytham

watched him as he scuttled to the boot of the car and began taking out a tin carpenter's box. Kenny was a mental case. Laytham shook his head. He must be nuts for even getting involved with him, let alone Hazard. And as for that fat prick, Donald . . .

'I'll wait, see if Donald appears. You go ahead.'

Kenny Graham didn't argue. The thought of setting up the explosives gave him a thrill almost sexual in its intensity – he loved it and even more he loved the sound, the BOOM! Then the orange whoosh! Fire. There was nothing to compare with it. Given the choice between a woman and setting a building alight, Kenny would go for the fire. He always had, ever since he was a little kid.

Laytham remained in the small, ill-lit side road, watching Kenny heading towards the factory. At one point he turned back and gave a big wanking gesture to the large 'Warning: Guard Dogs' sign. Ever since they had first started checking out the place, they had only ever seen one old boy.

Kenny used a jemmy to edge open the window on the ground floor. It opened more easily than he would have believed, almost causing him to drop the jemmy. Then he was inside, feeling the adrenalin pumping, his eyes darting and searching for the best location. *Inflammable*. He liked that word. Look for a nice inflammable area – boom, whoosh! Red hot orange flames.

Mike opened the main door, virtually dragging the terrified man inside. 'What in Christ's name you think you're playing at? You are one hour – AN HOUR – LATE! *What in hell's name are you playing at?*'

James Donald shook with terror, his jowled face shining with sweat. 'I'm sorry – it was my car, it overheated, I had to leave it at a garage. Then I couldn't find my wallet, I must have left it at home. I'm sorry, I didn't know whether to call you or not—'

Mike pulled the blinds closed, and watched as Donald mopped his face with a stained handkerchief.

15

'Did you do it?'

Donald was almost weeping. 'No. I was going to do it, then my car overheated. I was stuck in traffic and there's been some kind of accident up by the station – the police were all over the place.'

'Did you get to the factory?'

Donald shook his head, and blubbered that he was sorry, he had got scared, he'd dumped his car and walked to the yard.

Mike put his head in his hands. 'I don't believe I'm hearing this! *You walked here?*'

Donald nodded. His body odour was making Mike feel sick. 'Yes, I just told you, I must have left my wallet at home. I got no money, I can't even pick up the car. They said it was a leak. It boiled over, they were pouring some stuff into it—'

Mike interrupted, 'I don't give a fuck about your soddin' car! Did you or didn't you go to the factory and do what you were supposed to do?'

Shaking his head, Donald clutched at his raincoat pocket. 'I can't go on with this, it's all got out of hand, I never wanted to get in this deep. I can't deal with it. Just – you just pay me the money – that's all I want, I don't want to get in any deeper.'

Mike sighed, his fists clenched. So close, so close after months and months – and now this fat idiot was about to blow it all. Mike controlled the desire to throttle Donald, as he asked, almost as if he were addressing a child, if Donald had the disk ready. The man struggled with his pocket and produced a small hard computer disk, wrapped in a brown envelope.

'Yes, I've got it – but I can't do any more. I'm scared. Those two – they terrify me . . . They got Sherry – my wife's hysterical. This has got out of hand—'

Mike took the disk, held it loosely, staring at it, knowing that it was worth not just the months of work and arrangements, but thousands and thousands of pounds, and this fat, quaking fool was about to blow it – if he hadn't already done so.

'So you didn't, as you agreed, go to the factory. Right?'

Donald began to get tetchy. 'No, I didn't, I just told you. I don't want any trouble, my car—'

Mike grabbed him by the lapel of his stinking raincoat. 'You said, if I remember correctly, you wanted to get rich. *Right?* Well you're on the way to being very rich. All you had to do was get rid of the fucking evidence that ties you into it, and *you bleat about your fucking car overheating*!'

Donald pushed Mike away from him. 'Those two are madmen, they took my daughter, he took Sherry . . .'

Mike sighed, trying to piece everything together as Donald rambled on about his daughter running away from home, that his wife was going to call the police. Mike picked up the phone. He told Donald to dial his wife's number and tell her that on no account must she call the police, but that if she came in to see him then he would personally find their daughter, wherever she was, and bring her home. Just like he had the last time.

Donald spoke to his wife, darting scared looks at Mike as he told her not to worry about Sherry, Mike Hazard would trace her.

Mike flicked at the blinds, waiting until Donald replaced the phone, then battling to control his temper, he turned and smiled at the other man. 'Good. So we got Sherry all sorted out. Now, you and me will go to the factory. OK? You won't have to do anything but point me in the right direction.' Donald still hesitated. Mike wanted to throttle him. 'I'll be with you, OK? Just relax.'

'What about my car? It's stuck at that garage round the corner, that one near the main street.'

Mike sighed and took out one of his own business cards. He signed it on the back, and passed it to Donald. 'Give them this. Tell them I'll pay them in the morning. Go on. I'll meet you at the factory – go *on*, get moving.'

Donald clasped Mike's hand in gratitude. His hand felt wet and clammy. Then he handed over a set of keys. 'No, you do it – please, I can't take any more, I'm sick. Please. These are the keys to the back gates, the disks are in the small storage

17

room, first floor. Past the computer terminals, box with the same numbers, and they got the same writing on as this one. 'They're a batch from two years ago, that's why they got to be taken, they can be traced back to me – but I'm sick, Mike, this is making me ill.'

Hazard nodded, pocketed the keys and watched as Donald hovered and sweated at the door. 'OK, go on, get out.'

'Will I still get my cut? Mike?'

Mike nodded, tapping the disk in the brown envelope on the palm of his hand. 'Yeah, sure. Well, let's face it, without you none of us would be rich men, would we?'

Donald opened the door. 'I'll get the car, then. Will you call me tomorrow?'

Mike said he would, and waited until he saw Donald hurrying across the yard before he made up his mind where to hide the disk. Then he picked up the phone, dialled a number and waited. He had to wait almost seven ringing tones before his call was answered. He kept the conversation down to the minimum, his voice low and abrupt. 'The fat man is trouble. Perhaps he should be taken care of. He's scared, very scared.'

The voice at the other end of the line asked if the disk was ready. Mike said that it was, and the phone went dead.

Kenny Graham was sweating almost as much as Donald, but not with nerves. He stashed his equipment in the boot and slammed the lid down.

Laytham leaned out of the window. 'We got a problem. It's Donald. I just got a message. Get in the car, we got to go see him.'

Kenny stared. 'But it'll go up in fifteen minutes. Aren't we gonna stay and watch?'

Laytham gritted his teeth. 'Get in the car, Kenny. Get in the fuckin' *car – now!*'

Kenny Graham sat like a moody child as Laytham began to back the car down the narrow lane. 'The disk is ready,

Mike Hazard's got it. Donald is a problem. We sort him, then we have a talk with Hazard.

Mike Hazard arrived at the factory about four or five minutes after Laytham and Kenny had driven off. He left his car parked in the waste ground close to the factory, about a two-minute walk from the factory's rear fence. Using Donald's set of keys he opened the wire-meshed rear door. The gate displayed a large warning notice that the premises were patrolled by guard dogs. Donald had assured him that as far as he could tell even the alarm system was a fake.

Mike could see two or three men working on the lower ground floor. He kept on moving towards the rear of the building, and again used Donald's key to open a small fire exit door. He headed up the stairs and onto the second floor, easing open the door leading towards the computer sections, past row upon row of machines used to test the disks. He made two, or three wrong turns before he saw the stack of boxes awaiting shipment. He bent down, checking one after another, searching frantically for the odd box Donald had described. He had to work in the semi-darkness, not daring even to use a torch.

A smoke alarm suddenly broke the silence. The men working below immediately began to check out the lower storage section. As they opened a door into the filing office, an explosion ripped through the building. Within seconds fire began to rage through the factory. The main fire alarms shrilled and screamed, smoke billowing as two of the men tried to return back the way they had come. Thick black smoke, then a nightmare fireball engulfed them . . . While above, Mike Hazard tried to break the glass of the nearest window, his coat wrapped over his head. He smashed at the window as the flames and smoke gathered momentum. A second explosion tore the building apart.

The night security guard watched helplessly. The fire engines summoned, there was nothing he could do. Even from his position in the courtyard, the heat from the blazing building seared the hair on his head. He rushed to help a man who

19

emerged from the billowing smoke screaming that there were two more inside. They both saw the man on the second floor, silhouetted against the flames as he tried to clamber out onto the window ledge. His entire body seemed to be on fire.

Laytham returned from Hazard's office and leaned into the car. Kenny Graham was giggling. They could see the sky lit up from the burning factory. 'Look at that mother go! Look at it!'

Laytham slammed the car door shut and turned the engine. It was like being with a demented kid. He knew Kenny was a head case – now it was more than obvious as he shouted, pointing, wanting to know if they could at least drive past. 'Listen – *listen! That's the fire engines!*'

Laytham backhanded Kenny so hard he hunched against the side of the car, his mouth turned down like a thwarted child. They turned right over the small bridge from the boat-yard, and headed back on to the main Richmond road, passing the lit-up garage frontage, passing Donald as he stood on the pavement. Laytham swerved to a stop, and Donald stepped forward.

'I'm sorry . . . I had trouble with my—'

He never finished the sentence. Kenny was out fast, the back door of the car opened, and Donald's fat bulk was shoved inside. Laytham drove off, passing the mechanic who was still peering into the engine of Donald's car. The mechanic straightened and looked down to see water still pouring from the radiator. He turned to speak to Donald, but the big man had disappeared.

Kenny Graham, already worked up to a frenetic pitch, punched Donald in the belly. 'Where's the disk, you fat shit?'

Donald cringed against the back of the seat. 'I gave it to Mike. I swear to you, I don't have it. Mike – he's got it. It was finished last night. It's in his office!'

★

Susie woke early. She dressed and had a bowl of cornflakes before she called the office. There was still no reply, still the same answer machine message. She had waited long enough: whether Mike liked it or not she was going to see just what he was up to at that office.

She went down to the parking area, fingers crossed that none of the kids from the estate had twisted the aerial off during the night, or scratched the pristine white bodywork of the Volvo estate. Mike had bought it – well, it was on hire purchase – saying she needed a vehicle that would be easy to put a carry-cot and pushchair inside. The Volvo was intact, and Susie eased herself into the driving seat. It was difficult now for her to strap the safety belt round, as it was uncomfortable and restricting. She meant to write to the Government about pregnant women's safety belts. Probably the powers that be never realized that pregnant women are capable of driving.

It was just a short drive, but as she had only been to the yard once she checked the exact location on her road map.

Stella washed the breakfast dishes, cleaned the kitchen and wrote a note to the milkman that he need not deliver for the next few days. Checking her country pictures calendar again, she was really worried. She put on her coat, locked up the house, and yelled at the next door cat as he deposited his morning's load on her flower bed.

Stella had been to the agency twice. She checked the bus route, but missed the correct stop and had to walk back to the boatyard, crossing over the small bridge. She was flushed, her cheeks rosy red from her brisk walk. Noticing the pristine white Volvo parked in the Seekers Investigation bay, she made a mental note to tell Mike that if it wasn't a client's car he should put up a notice: 'Private Parking for Seekers Investigation Agency'. She looked up and saw through the half-open blinds that the light was on in the office. She pursed her lips. She was really going to let Mike have it.

CHAPTER TWO

Al Franks, wearing a pair of overalls and filthy sneakers, was about to start washing down the small reception area of the Seekers building. He worked at a very slow pace. He fetched the bucket, stood a while before remembering where he had stashed the floor cleaning fluid, then couldn't remember where the mop was. By the time he'd assembled all his equipment, he reckoned he should give the whole area a good sweep first, so it was a good fifteen minutes before he located the broom. The handle came away at the first brush. He spent further time looking for a roll of Sellotape which he then bound around the bottom of the broomstick. He stood banging it up and down on the floor to lodge it into the hole in the brush head.

Al had been given a small closet area that he could sit inside, with a view to the main entrance door. He had rescued an old easy chair from a rubbish tip, and a small shelf was filled with his magazines, the racing news and the morning's paper. He had his own large chipped mug, and placed behind the chair was a key rack: the keys to Seekers Investigation Agency, to the insurance broker on the same floor, the keys to the back doors and main entrance, and to the old boatyard. All were guarded by Al – when he was awake. But Al was usually to be found soundly asleep in his worn chair.

Susie woke him with such a start that he hit his head on the key rack.

'I'm Mrs Hazard. Could I have the spare keys to the agency?'

Al gaped. He had never met Suzie before, he was sure of that, and she was the sort you wouldn't forget. Moreover, she looked as if she was about to give birth at any moment. Al passed over the spare set of keys without a word, watching as she strode towards the small winding staircase that led up to the office floor. He half wondered if she would be able to manage the bend on the stairs.

'The reception could do with a clean. Are you the caretaker?'

Al nodded and scurried towards the closet for his cleaning equipment. It was something in her voice. He wondered why he had not met her before, but then he hadn't been 'resident caretaker' for that long. In fact, he was only supposed to be part time, just mornings, to open up and clean the offices. It had been Mike who had said he could be full time, Mike who had realized that the strange little man was desperate for work. It wasn't just the money aspect – he was paid a pittance. Rather, it was having some place to come to.

Al, his bulbous nose almost the size of his head, had a drink problem. He did try to keep it under control, but it was years since he had been regularly employed. He had dossed down all over London, a lonely, ugly little man with no family, no one he could ever make contact with: he had borrowed and he had stolen from every relative, until not one would give him the time of day. He had even spent a number of months in prison for vagrancy and small-time theft. An empty life loomed ahead for Al, until he had begged a few quid from Mike Hazard outside the Kingston Magistrates Court. That was how he had first met Mike, and they had struck up the odd conversation whenever Mike had been on a case. Mike had been surprised when a semi-spruce Al Franks had appeared at the boatyard. He had asked for a job, saying that anything would do, that he had now joined Alcoholics Anonymous, and was trying to straighten out his life. He had a room in a council house; he had been given a good suit and some extra clothes from the Salvation Army. His thinning hair plastered down over his forehead, his spaniel eyes and ridiculous nose obliterating most of his face touched Mike. Even though with only his office plus the insurance brokers who shared the building, a security-guard-cum-cleaner-cum-reception-area-manager-cum-caretaker wasn't really necessary, Al Franks was hired.

In his caretaker capacity, Al was brushing the reception

23

area when Stella appeared. She didn't pay much attention to him, but looked towards the key rack.

'Can I help you? I'm the new caretaker.' Al leaned on his wobbly broom, two strokes had exhausted him.

'Yes. I'm Mrs Hazard. Do you have the spare keys to my husband's office?'

'Pardon?'

Stella presumed that Al was deaf. She spoke louder. 'Mrs Hazard. I *need the keys*—'

'She's in the office, you want me to show you up?' Now Al was acting as reception manager, but Stella walked past heading towards the spiral staircase.

'I know the way, thank you.'

Al watched the rather pretty plump woman heading up the stairs. She had nice legs. 'I'm an alcoholic.'

Stella paused, looked down through the spiral staircase, unsure exactly what reaction the odd little man expected. 'Oh! Well, thanks for telling me. Is Mike upstairs?'

'Pardon?'

Stella continued up the staircase. Al's puzzled face watched her. He was sure that the other woman had said she was Mrs Hazard. Suddenly he felt like a wee dram, and scuttled to his bolt hole, muttering to himself that just a nip wouldn't hurt his programme.

Susie was in the office: drawers and filing cabinets were all open, and a few files had been thrown on the floor. The rubbish bin was overturned, and screwed-up papers littered the floor. She examined the stack of mail Al Franks had left on Mike's desk and began to check the dates. Some of the letters were a few days old. Taking a paper knife she slit open one envelope after another. Mostly circulars, and a couple of bills.

The office door was ajar. Stella pushed it wide open, looked around, then caught sight of Susie, whom she thought was the cleaner. She challenged her. 'You're taking a bit of a liberty, aren't you?'

Susie looked up. She, too, thought Stella was the cleaner.

'The place is a bit of a mess – the rubbish needs clearing out. Al Franks is supposed to clean—' Susie was interrupted.

'Oh, you're his wife!' Stella had concluded that Susie was married to Al, and she moved further into the office, heading towards the desk. 'He just told me,' she said, nodding her head. 'Alcoholic. I'm sorry . . . but you shouldn't be sorting out the mail. If you'd like to give it to me . . .'

Susie tapped the desk with the paper knife. 'I am *not* Al Frank's wife.'

'Oh, well. I'm sorry again.' Stella began to unbutton her coat, looking around for somewhere to hang it. 'Now I'm here you can leave the clearing up. I'll do it.'

'*What?*'

Stella grew a little tetchy. 'I said you can leave the office. Now that I'm here, give me the letters.'

Susie stared hard at Stella, then leaned forward, her hands covering her face. 'Oh, God, I'm so sorry. I didn't recognize you. It's Stella, isn't it?'

'Yes. Who are you?'

'Well, I'm Susie. I'm so sorry, we've never met, but I've seen a photograph of you.'

Stella moved closer to the desk, more than a little confused. 'Why? Who are you?'

'Susie. Mike must have told you about me.'

'No, no, he didn't. Do you work for him?'

Susie laughed. 'No, I'm his wife, I'm Susie.'

Now Stella laughed at the confusion. 'We got crossed wires love. *I*'m his wife, I'm Stella Hazard. So if you're cleaning the office, then sitting behind his desk going through his mail is not my idea of—'

'No, I'm *Susie*. We got married after your divorce.'

Stella, almost at the desk, took a quick step backwards. '*What?* Very funny. *I*'m his wife, so what the hell do you think you're playing at? Come on – out! This is no time for playing games.'

Susie was getting edgy. 'I'm not playing any game, *love*.' She stressed the last word. 'We've not met but I am Susie Hazard.'

25

Stella stared, unable to comprehend what on earth Susie was talking about.

'We got married after your divorce . . .' Susie rose from behind the desk. 'Would you like a cup of tea, or coffee?'

Only now could Stella see that Susie was pregnant. She gasped. 'What did you say?'

'Tea or coffee?'

'No, no, before that. You said, you said you—'

'Mike's wife, and, well, as you can see, we're about to have—'

Susie never got out the word 'baby'. Stella had to lean on the desk. 'Mike Hazard. We *are* talking about the same person?'

Susie laughed. 'Yes, Mike Hazard, and you *are* Stella. Yes?'

Stella nodded, her lips pressed into a tight thin line.

'Well, I am Susie. Mike and I married after your divorce, and the baby is due this month.'

Stella could only just manage to get the words out. She felt dizzy and breathless. 'Mike Hazard, the Mike Hazard that runs this agency, he's your husband?'

'Yes.' Susie nodded, then turned a photograph round on the desk: a photograph of herself with Mike. 'We got married.'

Stella's knees buckled, she seemed to disappear behind the front of the desk. 'Could you . . . get me a chair, quick . . . I'm going to faint.'

Susie rushed around the desk and pushed a chair from beside the filing cabinets towards Stella, who slumped back into the seat, and hung her head between her knees. She panted, 'This always happens . . . ever since I was sent to mixed infants school. Get a shock and I pass out like a light. I'm sorry, I think . . . I think I'm going . . .'

Stella fell forwards, her head clipping the desk before she slithered to the floor.

Al Franks hovered at the Seekers office doorway. Stella sat, all colour drained from her face, sipping a glass of water which Susie held out for her.

26

'Are you all right?' he asked.

Stella could only just manage a nod. She didn't know whether she was going to faint again, or be sick.

'Would you like a nip of brandy?'

'No, she's fine now, she's coming round.' Susie looked with concern as Stella slowly raised her head.

'Would you like a brandy, Stella?' Susie asked, but Stella slowly shook her head, and Susie wafted her hand for Al to leave.

Stella's voice seemed low, almost slurred. 'Was I hearing things, or did you say you were Mike's wife? Mike Hazard's wife?'

'You can go,' Susie said to Al, but he remained at the door. 'What's going on?'

'I am Mrs Hazard, everything is fine. Just shut the door.'

Al hesitated. He was sure the blonde, the one with her head between her knees, had said that she was Mrs Hazard.

'Er, I thought the other lady she was . . .'

Stella lifted her head and snapped, 'I am Mrs Hazard – now get out!'

Al returned to the booth for another quick nip from his flask as Kenny Graham appeared.

'Eh! Is Mike Hazard back yet?'

'No, I've not seen him for days.' Al sat back in his easy chair.

'So who's in the office?' Kenny demanded.

'Well, Mrs Hazard . . . and—'

'And?' snapped Kenny.

'Well, the other woman said *she* was Mrs Hazard. I dunno what's going on.'

Kenny clipped Al across the head, hard. 'Don't mess me about. You call this number as soon as he shows, understand?' He passed over a slip of paper, then leaned closer. 'Fifty quid now, you'll get another when you call me, OK?'

Al nodded. He didn't mind another clip over the head if it meant fifty quid in the hand. 'Yes, I'll call you.'

Kenny walked out. Al followed and watched him cross to the parked car, an old Mercedes. Someone was sitting in the driving seat, but with the odd nips he'd been taking, and without his glasses, Al couldn't make out who it was. The car screeched out of the boatyard and Al returned to his office. He pocketed the fifty-pound note, and opened the racing news: with his bonus from Kenny Graham he could have a little flutter on anything he fancied this afternoon.

Stella had recovered a little, but she still shook, her hands twisting a paper tissue round and round. She was trying to take everything in, but nothing seemed to make any sense. Susie sat behind the desk, equally stunned, but with far more composure. 'You never got a divorce?'

Stella licked her lips. 'No. There was no divorce.'

Susie breathed in and rubbed her tummy. 'Mike never divorced you?'

Stella snapped, 'I just said. He never divorced me. I think – look, there must be some mistake. I've never even heard of you. You've got it all wrong.'

Susie turned the photograph around. 'This is Mike, and this is me. It was taken on our wedding day, OK? He married me four and a half months ago.'

'You're pregnant!'

Susie sighed. 'That's a bit obvious, isn't it? I'm eight and a half months—'

'Is it Mike's?'

'Yes, it's Mike's. Look, let's keep calm, try and sort this all out. He told me he divorced you, now you are saying that isn't true. You were never divorced?'

'I am his wife! How many more times? He never even mentioned divorce, I've never heard of you . . . Oh, God! I'm going again . . .'

Stella bent forward and started panting for breath, it was all too much to take on board. She simply could not believe what she was hearing. Susie was beginning to feel a bit dizzy herself, she reached over and sipped at the glass of water.

28

'I worked with Mike at Stoke Newington.'

Stella's head jerked up. 'You're a police officer?'

'Yes – well, I was. I left with Mike when I got pregnant. We – well, it was a bit difficult for me to stay on. He wanted the baby, and . . . we moved out here to Richmond.'

'When? When did you move here?'

Susie chewed her lip. She was almost in tears. 'Six months ago.'

Stella panted. This couldn't be true. She pinched at her thigh; nothing was real, it was all unreal. She had moved to Richmond, the house – it was all some terrible mistake.

'I live in Richmond! We – we just bought a house here, we only moved a few months ago. You're saying that you live here as well?'

'Yes, we've got a council flat, just a few miles from the yard.'

'You live with Mike?'

'Yes.'

'Oh – dear God, I'm going again . . .'

Stella slumped forward, and Susie quickly crossed to the big street map pinned on the wall. 'Where? Where do you live?'

Stella dragged herself up, holding on to the edge of the desk. She stood next to Susie and pointed to the map. 'Here. This is our street.'

Susie pointed to the council estate. 'We live here.'

They stood side by side, staring in disbelief at the closeness of their addresses. Suddenly Susie felt the baby kick and she gripped Stella's arm. 'Get me to the chair. I think it's my turn now, I'm . . . I feel dizzy.'

Stella helped Susie to the chair she had just vacated and walked slowly round Mike's desk to sit in the old leather swivel chair. Mike's chair. They both felt it, the slow, awful, sickening realization of the lies, the terrible betrayal of their love and trust. But it was still so immediate, so confusing, that it left them stunned, unable to begin to comprehend the full implications of Mike's double life. He had spun such a web of deceit that not only was it difficult to believe but also impossible to accept.

'When did you last see him?' Susie asked.

Stella swallowed hard, clenching and unclenching her hands. 'Er, more than a week ago – in fact that's why I came here. I was getting worried . . .'

There was a long pause. Stella sighed, her voice strained. 'When did *you* last see him?'

Susie licked her lips. 'Over a week. That's why *I* came here as well, I was getting—' She never completed the sentence, her admission that, like Stella, she too was worried. She leaned over and switched on the answer machine. They both sat listening to each other's messages repeated over and over, until Stella turned it off unable to listen to her own voice – and Susie's voice – any more. Their calls to Mike, each of them worrying, were just further confirmation that this was not some terrible mistake – but reality.

'Something is wrong,' Susie said, softly.

'I would say that was the understatement of the year!' Stella retorted. 'If he was to walk in that door right now I think I'd take this paper knife and kill him!'

Susie pushed herself up out of the chair and scanned the office. 'I think this place has been searched. Every drawer was open when I came in.'

Stella looked around. 'He's not the tidiest of men—' Then she had to turn away, her face creased with emotion. She couldn't stop the tears. 'How could he do this? Why?'

Susie, on the verge of tears herself, sniffed hard. 'He could get arrested for bigamy – he must be insane! Why on earth didn't he tell me the truth? *Why*? I can't believe he would do this to me.'

'*You* can't?' Stella retorted, fishing in her pocket for a handkerchief. 'I'll bloody punch him so hard, the *bastard*!' Being angry helped. Stella stood up, hands on her hips. 'Where's his diary? Let's find out where the bugger is, I'll get the law on him. If my father was alive he'd shoot him – I'll shoot him, never mind my poor father. He'd turn in his grave if he knew.'

Susie flicked through Mike's diary. There was no entry for the past week, in fact longer. She snapped the diary closed.

'You don't think – I mean, what if it suddenly all got too much for him and he's just taken off? Do you think that's what he's done?'

Stella was at the wall map, tracing the short distance between their two homes. 'My God, he must have walked between homes, come to me from seeing you! How could I never have even suspected?'

Susie gave a short, mirthless laugh. '*You* never suspected, what about me? I was a police officer. What about his car, have you seen his car?'

Stella shook her head, then looked at the floor, the overturned waste basket, the filing cabinets. 'Maybe you're right, maybe the place has been searched. If he was able to run two homes and neither of us knew why just up and run? I mean . . . How was he, the last time you saw him?'

Susie shut her eyes, recalling how he had lovingly touched her belly and kissed her. 'He was . . . nothing unusual about him. And you?'

Stella remembered him slipping his arms around her waist as she dried the breakfast dishes. 'He was . . . like he always was, didn't seem worried. In fact, he was talking about some big job.'

'Yes, he told me he was doing a big job as well. Do you know *any*thing about it?'

Stella shook her head. Susie tapped the desk, then passed over Stella's handbag. 'I think something has happened. Come on.'

'Where are we going?'

'Police station. I'm going to report him missing.'

Before Stella could reply, or snap that if anyone should report Mike Hazard missing it should be her, as she was his wife, Susie was walking down the corridor towards the stairs.

Al Franks was confronted by Susie and Stella. 'When did you last see Mr Hazard?'

Al had almost finished his flask. 'Pardon?'

'I said, when did you last see Mike Hazard?'

31

Al looked at Stella and then back to Susie. 'Are you Mrs Hazard?'

Both women answered at the same time. 'Yes.'

Al Franks hunched his shoulders. He knew he couldn't be seeing double – one woman was black, the other white, and one was pregnant.

'Pardon?' he slurred.

Susie repeated the question as Al screwed up his face and attempted to recall the last time he had seen Mike Hazard. All he could think was that it had been quite a while, maybe more than a week, but the exact number of days was hazy. During that time he'd had a little bother. In fact, he was about to head for some more as he was obviously drinking again.

Susie tried to get some sense out of him, but Stella tapped her arm. 'I don't think he can see straight, let alone think straight. I can smell the drink from here.'

Susie pointed to Al. 'You sober up, Mr Franks, you're supposed to be the caretaker. Go and get some coffee, and if – if you see Mike Hazard, will you tell him we were here? Both of us!'

Al watched as they walked out. He searched in his pockets for the scrap of paper Kenny Graham had given him, then decided against calling until he had had, as Susie suggested, some strong, very strong, black coffee.

Susie opened her bag for the car keys as she headed towards the white Volvo estate. Stella gaped. 'Is this yours?'

'It's on HP. Get in.'

Stella shut the car door, and heaved the safety belt round. 'Well, it's not a colour I'd choose, it'll show every mark. I paid half the money towards Mike's car, but he's never let me drive it. I use the bus. What sort of car is this, then?'

Susie drove out of the boatyard. 'It's a Volvo, Stella, and like I said it's on HP. I don't own it. Now where's the local police station?'

Stella shrugged, she had no idea. Susie gestured to the glove compartment. 'There's an *A to Z* in there, check it out.'

'What street is it in? I don't know what to look up.'

Susie stopped the car at traffic lights and wound down her window. She called across to a pedestrian. 'Police station?'

The man pointed to the top of the road, and said it was first on the right. Susie waved a thank you. 'OK, better let me do the talking, Stella – OK if I call you Stella? – but it'll be best because I know all the procedures.'

'You mean you'll tell them he's a bigamist?'

Susie flashed a look at Stella, surprised at her stupidity. 'No, Stella. I am going to report him missing . . . possibly in suspicious circumstances.'

Stella gave an odd half-laugh. 'I'd say they were suspicious. I'd like him arrested, but before they get him, I'd like a go at him – and if it's all right with you, *I*'ll report him missing. I'm his legitimate wife – and a woman in your condition should wear her seat belt! *If* you don't mind me saying so.'

The young uniformed police officer took great pains listening to Stella as she tried to explain why she wanted her husband reported missing. She was very hesitant about Susie's connection in the matter, but in fact it was Susie, rather than Stella, who worried him, because she refused to sit down. She was so obviously heavily pregnant that the young officer was scared she might go into labour there and then.

'I haven't heard from him, you see, for nine days, and, well, there are a few circumstances that, well . . . he always calls. I'm used to him being away for maybe two or three days a week, but . . .'

The officer looked to Susie. 'Are you sure you wouldn't like to sit down?'

'Quite sure. And we'd like to fill in a missing persons report.'

The officer gave a condescending smile. 'All in good time. I just need to ascertain a few more details. You are?'

'Mrs Hazard,' Susie said, with a glittering look to Stella.

'Ah, I'm sorry. I'm confused. I thought this lady was Mrs Hazard?'

33

Susie gritted her teeth. 'We both are.'

'*I*'m his wife!' said Stella firmly. 'I'll give you the details.'

The officer gave a brief smile – it reminded him of one of those comedy shows – and turned back to Stella. 'But there is just one Mr Hazard, correct?'

'Yes!' they both replied, and looked daggers at each other.

'And you are *both* married to this, er . . . Mike Hazard? Is that correct?'

Susie suddenly leaned against the counter. 'Will you please just take the details? I have a photograph and—'

Now Stella leaned into the counter. 'He's my husband. We live at—'

'One moment,' the officer interrupted as he searched for the correct form, every move slow and methodical. Susie passed the photograph to him. She began to reel off age, height, build, office address, home address . . . Stella interjected with the second home address. That was when the young officer looked up and smiled broadly. 'So he has two wives after him! One might be bad enough, but two—'

Stella hit the counter with the flat of her hand. 'Just you take that smile off your face, sonny, this is not funny. And this woman here is a police officer. She'll report you. Just take down the particulars.'

The officer wrote in silence, then looked at Stella. 'You said: "There are a few circumstances . . .". What did you mean by that?'

Susie glanced at Stella, then answered for her. 'We think, we can't be certain, but his office looked disturbed, filing cabinets opened, all the desk drawers too. It looked as if someone had been searching it, the wastebin was turned over, but there was no damage – well, not so far as I could ascertain.'

The officer nodded. 'This is Seekers Investigation Agency, yes? And Mr Hazard is a private investigator, yes?' He smiled again. It was getting funnier by the second. He coughed, attempting to hide his expression. 'Are there any items of clothing missing?'

The women looked at each other.

'Have you checked?'

They both shook their heads, then Stella said that Hazard's

34

car was missing. The officer enquired, po-faced, if they had the registration number. Stella couldn't recall it, but Susie reeled it off, together with the year and make of the old BMW. All was carefully noted down.

'Right, that seems to be everything. I suggest you both check to see if any items of clothing are missing, suitcases, and if so, perhaps you would let us know. In the meantime I will give it twenty-four hours before we officially—'

Susie stared at him. 'This is official right now. He's made no contact for nine days.'

The officer raised an eyebrow. Pregnant she may be, but she seemed as hard as nails. 'Please call the station if you discover anything missing.'

As the two women walked out, the officer turned to his sergeant, just appearing with two mugs of tea. He wafted the form in front of him. 'You want to hear what I've just been through. You ever heard of a Seekers Investigation Agency? Seems the investigator's done a bunk, leaving not one, but two wives.'

The sergeant put down his mug. 'Is this a joke?'

Stella and Susie walked towards the Volvo. Suddenly Susie felt tired, her whole body began to shake. 'I think . . . you'd better drive, Stella. I feel dizzy.'

Stella took the proffered car keys. 'Little twerp in there – you should have told him to get a superior in. He didn't take us seriously.'

Susie slumped into the passenger seat. 'Well, first we'd better do as he said. Maybe we did jump the gun a bit. You check if any of Mike's clothes are missing.'

'What are you going to do?'

Susie sighed. She was feeling terrible. 'The same, of course – what do you think? If, as he said, stuff's missing, especially suitcases, then you'd better call me.'

Stella shot out of the parking space and, jerked backwards, Susie grabbed at the seat belt. She didn't say a word throughout the short drive, as Stella overtook everything on the road, indicated left and whipped into a right turn. Eventually they entered the council estate, and Susie gasped out directions to her block. She closed her eyes as Stella drove into the parking space too fast, slamming on the brakes. Slowly Susie unclipped her seat belt. 'Stella, have you ever taken a driving test?'

Stella flung the driving door shut and locked the car. 'Yes, but Mike hardly ever let me drive. Here.' She tossed over the keys and looked around. 'Well, this isn't exactly what I'd call desirable. Are these council?'

'Some,' said Susie, 'but a lot of residents have bought theirs. We just rent.' The use of the word 'we' made Stella smart.

'I can walk home or get the bus. *We* have a small terraced house.' But she didn't continue, she waved her hand. 'You'd better give me your phone number.'

In silence Susie jotted down her number and Stella passed over hers. She slipped Susie's phone number into her handbag. 'If Mike's at home I'll get him to call you. Maybe shut him in the wardrobe and chuck the key away.'

Susie felt dizzy again. She wanted to go and lie down, wanted to get away from Stella and her half-hearted jokes.

Stella walked away, paused and looked back at the white Volvo. 'You get a new Volvo. Me? I get a food mixer. Call me anyway, will you?'

Susie nodded, already heading up the concrete stairs to the first-floor landing. Stella's jokes. The reference to the food mixer wasn't funny. She seemed almost tragic, standing there clutching her handbag to her body.

Stella waited for the bus on automatic pilot, paying the fare, getting off and walking down the street. She banged the gate open and pushed at the front door. Not until she had slammed it behind her did she break down. Slowly she slithered down the wall, like a rag doll, and wept. Sobbed and sobbed. Her whole body shook as she cried. She didn't know how long she sat in the hall, half an hour or an hour, but she remained there until there were no more tears, then she kneeled forward and pulled herself up onto her feet. Still half crouched, she glanced into the lounge, and then she straightened and pushed open the door wide.

'Oh, my God!' Every cushion, every single item in the room

had been hurled around – the sofa cushions slit open, the drawers dragged out, even the carpets had been rolled up, and every picture thrown off the wall.

The kitchen was a sea of broken crockery. Again, every drawer, every cupboard had been wrenched open. The bedrooms were the same – the whole house had been wrecked. As if in a trance, Stella moved from room to room, then panic rose inside her, and she started panting, panting, about to faint as she scrabbled at her dressing table frantically searching for her jewellery box. She found it thrown on the floor, its contents intact. Not that she had much, but the bracelets and necklaces were strewn over the floor. She crawled around retrieving each item.

The wardrobe doors were open, all Mike's clothes had been tossed aside, shirts, jackets, trousers and ties. She stood in the centre of the room, surrounded by debris. She couldn't cry, she was in a state of total shock. 'Oh, God, oh, my God.'

Susie had the keys in her hand, about to unlock the front door of the flat, when she realized it was already open. She pushed it wider. 'Mike? *Mike?*'

The first thing she saw was the pram she had brought home, sitting in the tiny hallway. 'Mike? Mike, are you here? *Mike?*'

Susie listened. Silence. She moved cautiously towards the small kitchen dining area, and pushed the door open. The entire room was wrecked. She was about to step further into it when she heard the sound of breaking glass coming from the direction of the bedroom. 'Mike? *Mike, is that you?*'

She never saw him. The blow to the back of her neck stunned her and she slumped to her knees. Her first thought was for her baby and she instinctively wrapped her arms around her belly to protect herself. She fell face forward, slamming her head against the side of the door frame. Curled up tight, she repeated over and over, 'Please take whatever you want. Don't, don't hurt my baby.'

The foot in the filthy two-toned sneaker swung back and kicked her in the ribs. She screamed and screamed as the kicks came in rapid succession. Still she wouldn't release her arms from around her belly, too afraid that the kicks would injure her baby. The kicks seemed to last for ever. Then she blacked out.

Stella stepped over the debris to get to the phone. She had to throw cushions aside until she found it, torn from the wall. She turned frantically this way and that, searching for her handbag, then she dashed out into the street. First she rushed to the young couple's house next door, and rang the doorbell continuously, but they were still at work. She tried the house on the other side, but her stupid neighbour wouldn't even come to the door.

'Open the door! I have to call the police. *Open the door! I have to call the police!*'

Eventually Stella succeeded in getting someone to answer their front door, and she gasped out that she'd been burgled. A patrol car arrived fifteen minutes later. The telephone was plugged back into the wall, the connection having simply been torn from its socket. It was almost an hour before the police left, saying they would send someone to take fingerprints and not to touch anything. They advised her to contact her insurance brokers, and try to assess all the damage and what had been stolen.

The strange part was that nothing seemed to have been taken, but until everything had been put back in order Stella couldn't really be sure if anything was missing.

She hadn't checked Mike's clothes or suitcases, and it was not until after the police had left that she thought to call Susie. There was no answer; the phone seemed to be disconnected. Stella asked the operator to check if there was a fault on the line, and they called back to say that there was no mechanical fault, perhaps the phone had been left off the hook.

Stella could direct the taxi driver to the flats, but couldn't remember the flat number. In the event, she recognized the white Volvo still parked in the bay outside. Still she didn't know which flat, but told the taxi driver to wait as she hurried up the steps where she had last seen Susie. Stella moved along the landing corridor, checking each front door, then she caught sight of the door to number fourteen left ajar. She looked at the bell; there was no name, so she gently pushed the door wider open. 'Susie? Susie?'

Stella glimpsed the pram overturned in the doorway, and then she saw Susie's body, hunched by the doorframe. Blood was streaming down her face as she attempted to stand, her arms clasped around her belly. 'Help me, help me – the baby . . . the baby.'

Siren screaming, the ambulance drew up outside Kingston Hospital's Emergency section. As Susie was carried out on a stretcher, she seemed very disorientated, saying over and over again that she was losing her baby. Stella, looking on as they took Susie into the emergency department, stood with her coat stained with blood, her hand aching where Susie had clung to her. The hospital reception called her over: they needed all the relevant information on Susie. It was then that Stella started panting. Unable to get her breath, she tottered forward, and a nurse hurried towards her.

'Are you all right?'

'No, I need a chair – I'm going to faint.'

CHAPTER THREE

Stella sat with a blanket around her, clasping a mug of tea. The registrar was taking details. There was some confusion when Stella gave Susie's name as Susie Hazard, and then, as she had already told them that she was Mrs Stella Hazard, they enquired if she was Susie's mother. Stella shook her head. 'No, I'm not her mother.'

'Do you know any of her relatives?'

'No.'

'What about her husband?'

Stella sipped the tea. 'His name is Mike. Mike Hazard.'

'Do you know where he can be contacted?'

'No, no, I don't. He's missing, we've not seen him for eight days.'

'Do you know if Mrs Hazard has any allergies?'

'No. I only met her today. Is she all right? I mean – the baby, is it all right?'

A plump, sweet-faced nurse appeared. 'Mrs Hazard? Your daughter's going to be fine. A doctor's with her now, she's asking to see you.'

'I'm not her mother.'

The nurse looked to the registrar. 'Oh, I'm sorry. She's asking for Mrs Hazard . . . She's gone into labour.'

Stella stood up. 'She's having it now?'

The nurse smiled. 'Yes, she's fine. It'll be a while yet, but we've put her in a side ward. Do you want to see her?'

Stella was led into the small private room. The injury to Susie's head had been cleaned and she wore a small plaster covering it. Her eyes were closed, her belly seemed enormous.

The sweet-faced nurse drew up a chair, and smiled. She's a little drowsy. The contractions are a good distance apart, could be quite a long wait. Can I get you another cup of tea?'

Stella shook her head, sitting down uneasily by the bed. The nurse crept out and closed the door. Susie lay peacefully, the starched white sheets across her chest, her elegant long, tapering hands resting on the coverlet. Only now did Stella really look at her, and in the quietness of the room, she half rose to study Susie's face. Her thick black eyelashes were like a small child's, so long they seemed to rest against her high chiselled cheekbones. She had a perfect nose, full lips. Susie's youth touched something inside Stella. She was very beautiful – no wonder Mike had fallen in love with her. She was like a gazelle, apart from the huge swollen belly.

Stella reached out, stroking the mound with a feather-like touch. Mike's child was in there, maybe even his son. The pain was sharp, like a punch to her heart. How many years had she dreamed of waiting in the hospital maternity ward, about to have the child she had longed for – had prayed for? And now, here she was, sitting, watching and waiting for another woman to have Mike's baby.

The nurse returned and gestured for Stella to join her, as two police officers wanted to talk to her. Stella crept out, easing the door closed behind her.

The two young uniformed officers were a bit embarrassed as heavily pregnant women tottered past the small room the matron had directed them to. They had been told that Susie had been mugged, and her flat ransacked. They had already sent someone to secure the flat, but now they needed to know more facts. Stella was really unable to tell them anything further. She hadn't seen anyone near the flat, didn't know what had occurred at all. They were aware that Stella had reported a burglary the same afternoon; did she think there could be a connection? Again, Stella could give no insight into why they had both been robbed, and she hadn't seen anyone in her house. She hesitated before mentioning that both she and Susie had been to the local Richmond police station earlier that day.

The officer made jottings in his notebook, then looked up. 'Why was that?'

'I – well, we – reported my husband missing. Mike Hazard.'

The young officer wrote copiously in his notebook, before looking up again. 'Er, I'm sorry. I'm a bit confused. Is it your husband missing or Mrs Susie Hazard's?'

Stella coughed, and pulled at her coat. 'Er, well, he's my husband, but he, well, he lives with . . .'

'Ah, I see.'

Stella looked at the young fresh-faced officer. 'No, I don't think you do. But I can't give you any more details.'

She remained in the room, sitting staring up at the wall. The police had left – at least *they* didn't find the situation amusing. Maybe Susie had been right, maybe something really was very wrong. The robberies, Mike's disappearance – it couldn't all be coincidence, could it? Would Mike really have just upped and left? Had his lies and deceit eventually made him just pack up and leave? Maybe he owed somebody money . . . So many maybes and unanswered questions. Stella felt tired and, more than that, desperately lonely. She could think of no one to whom she could turn, no one she could tell what was happening in her life. The overwhelming realization that there wasn't anyone, not even one close female friend, she could talk to, no relative. Even the few friends she did have, how could she try to discuss with them what had happened. Mike had been her whole life. Suddenly she felt scared.

The nurse, the plump girl with the lovely china blue eyes, peeked around the door, then carried in a cup of tea. 'I thought you may be needing a cuppa by now. My name's Doreen, by the way.'

Stella took the cup of tea, grateful for the girl's friendliness, and her eyes filled with tears. Doreen put her arms around her.

'Don't you worry now, she's going to be fine. Come on and sit with her. The baby's heartbeat is strong, and the contractions are coming every five minutes, so it won't be as long as we thought.'

Once again Stella took up her bedside vigil. The cup shook as she replaced it on the saucer.

Susie opened her eyes. 'Oh, thank goodness. I've asked and asked for you.'

'Well, I'm here now. I had to talk to the police, get everything sorted.'

Susie nodded. 'It hurts like hell.'

'Is there somebody I can call? Have you got someone?'

Susie moaned, her face twisted. Stella leaned over her. 'Can I call someone – your mother? Susie?'

Susie moaned again. 'No, no, there's no one. Ohhhhh, Ohhhhhhh . . .' She grabbed Stella's hand and held it tightly as pain tore through her. Stella was almost hauled off her feet. Susie yelled again, and struggled to sit up. 'Why don't they do something? *Ohhhhhhhhhhh* . . .'

Stella remembered all the pregnancy books she'd read. 'Keep calm. Breathe steadily while you've got the pain . . . Slowly.'

Doreen appeared, checked Susie, felt her belly, and looked at Stella. 'That's good, just keep talking to her. If you need me just press the bell, I'll be back in the ward.'

Stella nodded, Susie thrashed around and then sighed as the contraction eased. Still she wouldn't let go of Stella's hand.

'Mike wouldn't have walked out. He wanted the baby, Stella, he wanted the baby. Something's wrong, Mike wanted the baby.'

Stella patted Susie. 'Yes, yes, I know, love. Now you just try and relax, and keep breathing nice and steady. Could you just let my hand go a bit, my arm's going blue. Susie? Come on, love, nice deep breaths. I know all about having babies. I had three miscarriages, you know, very early on. I mean, I never got to this stage but I had a phantom pregnancy once. God! I blew up like a balloon. Breathe – *Susie, let go of my hand!*'

The next contraction began and as the pain intensified Susie gave an ear-splitting yell. Stella frantically pressed at the bell and Doreen reappeared.

'My God, I feel as if I'm having this baby myself! She's pulling me all over the place.'

Doreen leaned over Susie. 'Now, you be a good girl. The doctor will be coming in soon, and—'

Susie let rip again, and Doreen lifted the covers, felt her stomach, then drew them up. She looked at Stella. 'Doing nicely.'

'No, I'm not. It's coming now!' Susie struggled up.

Doreen plumped up her pillows, easing Susie back. 'Everything's fine. Just try and relax.'

Stella fetched a glass of water and held it out for Susie, but another contraction started, so hard that she was crying. Doreen left the door ajar, and gestured for Stella to push the button if she was needed.

Once again Susie grabbed Stella, this time so forcefully that she was half-way across the bed. 'I'm sorry. I'm so sorry, Stella, I'm so sorry.'

'Now, don't be silly, don't you think about me, you just concentrate on that baby. That's a good girl. Let go of my arm, that's it, now we'll do it together. Deep breath through the nose, that's it . . . You know I had a room all ready, all decorated for the baby, little pink elephants and rabbits. Well, the only baby I got was my father. He had this heart attack, you see, so he moved in . . . Well, he was a drinker, we had a shocking time with him. One night he started yelling that he was seeing things climbing up the wall, I said to him, "You soft bugger, they're elephants!" And he shouted at me, yelled at the top of his voice, "You stupid bitch, since when have elephants been pink?" I said to him "These ones are pink, and the blue things are rabbits." '

Ten minutes later Susie's waters broke. Stella was hoarse, her arms black and blue from Susie's frantic clutches. At last the doctor and nurses reckoned it was time to take her through to the delivery room, but she wouldn't let go of Stella.

'Don't leave me . . . *Stella* . . .'

Susie's loud bellowing voice could be heard right down the corridor as she was wheeled towards the delivery room. Swearing and abusive, at one point she demanded they let her go home, and then there was silence. Stella, already tired, felt completely drained now, like a limp rag.

Doreen returned, and grinned. 'She's got the whole ward up. What a temper! They often give the poor doctor a punch, all different, but she's as strong as an ox!'

Stella nodded, rubbed her arms. 'Yes. Don't I know it. There won't be any complications, will there?'

Doreen chuckled. 'Not with that one. Now, do you want another cuppa before I go into the delivery room?'

Stella shook her head. 'I need a cigarette, I don't suppose you can smoke in here, can you?'

Doreen winked. 'No smoking zone. But there's one room. Come on, I'll have a quick drag myself. It's nicknamed the Poll Room – pollution!'

Stella had a cigarette; she only normally smoked the odd one or two. She even thought about calling Beryl from the Bake O Bread as she knew she wouldn't make it to work the next day. She'd have to clean up, but at least it would give her something to do. She wondered where all the insurance policies were; they'd need new curtains, cushions. They? She stubbed out her cigarette. Where the hell was he? she wondered. Had he . . . Stella tried to recall the right word, the one the police used for missing persons. Ah . . . she remembered it: absconded. Had he, she wondered, absconded? It was still too much for her to take in. What a day. She tipped the contents of the ashtray into the bin, and buttoned up her coat. Doreen appeared.

'Come on, come on. It's a boy, eight and a half pounds!'

Stella followed Doreen to the nursery, the newborn babies in their row of cots, like a shop window for the relatives and friends to see. Doreen waved to Stella, then reached over into one of the cots, and gently lifted the perfect sleeping newborn boy. He had a thick thatch of black curly hair, so thick it was hard to believe he was so young, so newly born.

Stella rested her hands against the glass, pressing her face closer. Doreen wore a surgical mask, but her blue eyes sparkled, and she held the baby higher for Stella to get a good clear view of him.

'Mike always wanted a son,' she whispered. The tears welled up, spilling down her cheeks. 'Oh, God. How I wanted one, too . . .'

Doreen gently lowered the baby back in his cot, wrapping

the blankets close and tight. When she straightened up and turned round, Stella had gone.

Stella's hands dug deep in her coat pockets. The air was cold. She hadn't taken a taxi; instead she walked, needing the fresh air, afraid to go home. As she turned the corner into her road, we saw the police patrol car and the panic started. She began to run.

She called out for them to wait, afraid they would drive away. 'Have you found him?'

The officer turned. This one wasn't in uniform, in fact he was quite attractive. 'Mrs Hazard?' Detective Inspector Richard Levy asked quietly.

Stella nodded. 'Yes. Have you found my husband? Is it about Mike?'

'No, no, I'm sorry. It's about a BMW registered to a Michael Hazard of this address. I wondered, if it's not too inconvenient, if you would come with us.'

'Why? Is something wrong with it?'

'No.' Levy smiled as he opened the rear passenger door. 'We just need to ask you a few questions, nothing to get worried about. If you'd prefer it, I can come round in the morning.'

'No, I don't mind.' She allowed herself to be helped into the back seat.

As they drove off, his colleague at the wheel, Levy turned to Stella as he fastened his safety belt. 'You heard from your husband at all?'

'No. No. Is something wrong?'

Levy shook his head. 'No, I just wondered. You did fill in a missing persons report, and then, with his car being also reported missing . . . sort of coincidence . . . ?'

'Well, you were looking for it, weren't you?'

Levy turned back to Stella again. 'Pardon?'

'I said, you were looking for his car, weren't you?'

Levy faced front. 'No, not exactly. Do you know if he often parked it in the Norbiton area?'

Stella said she had no idea where he parked it.

'Been missing nine days? Yes?'

Stella was starting to feel very uneasy. 'You mean Mike? My husband?'

Levy turned yet again to face her in the back seat. 'No, his car. When did you last see his car?'

Stella ran her hands through her hair. 'Well, I suppose when I last saw him. Nine days ago.'

Levy nodded. They had a witness who had stated that the BMW had been left close to the factory for possibly two days. Levy was heading the investigation into the factory fire. Arson was suspected. He did not repeat this to Stella, but gave a small snide look at the driver. The missing persons report had indeed been looked over by Levy and the fact that two wives had reported Hazard missing caused quite a few laughs. They presumed one to be the ex-wife, unaware of the bigamy implications. Hazard, he suspected, had simply done a runner. But the discovery of the car so close to the factory, and then the contents of the boot, had caused Levy to change his mind.

He had run a check on Mike Hazard and his so-called investigation agency. He discovered that Hazard was an ex-police officer. What Levy had subsequently been told about him left a nasty taste in his mouth. No officer likes to hear about one of their own turning crooked, and word was that Mike Hazard had been taking bribes and doctoring evidence. Maybe, Levy mused, that was why he could afford to have two women.

Stella walked into the police pound, Levy slightly ahead of her. A uniformed officer accompanied them, and one was standing waiting by the BMW.

'Is this your husband's car, Mrs Hazard?'

Stella nodded. She didn't even have to look at the number plate. She recognized the dented wing and the big scratch from one end to the other on the driver's side, another thing Mike was always intending to get repaired.

'Yes, that's our car.'

'Do you have a key to the boot?' Levy asked.

'No. I don't have keys to the car. I don't drive it very often.'

Levy signalled for the boot to be opened and gestured for Stella to move closer. 'Do you recognize this holdall?'

Stella nodded. It was a black leather one she had bought from the catalogue for Mike last Christmas. The officer unzipped the holdall, and held the bag open.

She gasped. The bag bulged with bundles and bundles of bank-notes.

'You know anything about the contents of the holdall?' Levy asked.

Stella shook her head. 'No, no.'

Sipping at yet another cup of tea, Stella was now seated in Detective Inspector Levy's office. She crossed her legs uncomfortably. She badly needed to go to the lavatory; also she hadn't eaten all day. Her bladder felt as if it were bursting. 'I need to go to the ladies.'

A female officer ushered Stella out. Levy lit a cigarette and turned to his young sergeant. The bag was placed on the table. Inspector Kent's immaculate sports jacket and grey flannels irritated Levy. They'd both been on duty since eight that morning and he looked and felt crumpled, but Kent seemed fresh as a daisy.

'How much?'

'There's twenty thousand. Used notes.'

'Anything else?'

'No, just the cash.'

Levy drew on his cigarette. 'Can we interview the bloke at the hospital yet?'

Kent shook his head. 'Doc said maybe tomorrow, he's suffering from smoke inhalation and first degree burns to his chest and hands, hair's singed off and one ear.—' He stopped talking as Stella returned.

Levy smiled, proffering a cigarette. As Stella took one, he noticed her hands were shaking. 'You feeling all right, Mrs Hazard?' He struck a match.

Stella inhaled. 'I'm fine, it's been . . . well, it's been quite a day, and night.'

Levy nodded, watching as she sipped at the cold tea. 'There's twenty thousand pounds in your husband's holdall.'

Stella nearly choked on the tea. '*What?*'

'Twenty thousand. Do you know why your husband would have that amount of cash in the car?'

Stella couldn't believe it. 'Twenty thousand? Are you sure?'

Levy assured Stella that they were absolutely certain, and made it very clear that an officer had been with the car ever since it had been discovered. He then asked casually if she knew anything about Thompsons Computers factory. Stella seemed nonplussed.

'Thompsons Computers factory caught fire, two nights ago. You know it? Did you read about the fire?'

She shook her head.

'Two men died, another is—'

Stella interrupted, 'What has this got to do with my husband's car?'

'It was parked close to the factory, on some wasteground at the rear of the main building. Thompsons Computers factory. Do you know if your husband was involved with anyone from there, or would have been there recently?'

Stella shook her head. 'I've never heard of it. He may have been working for them, I don't know.' She replaced the cup and saucer on the desk. 'That money in my husband's car, is it mine? I own part of the car, it's my car. So does that mean whatever's in the car is mine?'

Levy nodded, watching her closely. 'Or the property will be yours, when it's released.'

She frowned. 'I don't understand.'

Levy arched his fingers together. 'Well, we have a missing persons report on your husband, and obviously until we are satisfied there are no suspicious circumstances relating to your husband's disappearance we will have to retain the contents of his vehicle, and the car itself, until we are – well – satisfied it can be released.'

'To me?' Stella asked.

'Yes, if you can prove ownership. But we want to run some

tests first, check out a few things. Shouldn't take too long, we'll let you know as soon as you can collect it. Meanwhile, I suggest you go home, and we'll be in touch.'

Levy stood up, indicating that the interview was over. Almost as an afterthought he asked Stella to let them know immediately if her husband should make contact. He then told Kent to make sure a car took Stella home. He checked his watch, tired. It had been a long day and it was now after eleven o'clock.

Stella, half turned in the doorway. 'Twenty thousand pounds?'

Levy nodded, and repeated, 'Twenty thousand pounds.'

Stella sat in silence in the rear of the patrol car as she was driven home. 'Twenty thousand pounds.' She kept on seeing the figure in her mind. Starting to put two and two together, she came up with a lot more than four: her imagination ran riot. Maybe Mike was planning to move away with Susie; she'd said they just rented the flat. Was that what the money was for? Her lips tightened, she knew if he had laid his hands on that amount it was her money. The cash her dad had left. Had he lied about how much the boatyard office cost, the house? Just how many lies had he told? She even wondered if Susie knew more than she had said. She had been in the office sorting through the mail – what if they were in it together?

The officer offered to walk Stella to her front door, but she didn't seem to hear him. She kicked open the front door. As she looked over the debris that filled her house, she remembered Susie, how she had almost lost the baby. Her brain felt as if it were going to explode. She felt like punching someone, anyone, but instead she just threw off her coat, forcing herself not to sink under the weight of the nightmarish day she had just lived through.

She started there and then, cleaning, washing, putting the house back to order. She worked all through the night. She was carrying out big black rubbish bags to the dustbins when she spotted next-door's cat, at it again. She yelled at it. The

50

cat, caught mid-squat, shot back over the fence.

Stella had no idea of the time. She was just about to get a fresh bucket of water when the phone rang. It was Beryl from the Bake O Bread wondering if Stella was coming in as she was late already and the manageress would make her appearance any minute.

'I'm not coming in today, Beryl. I've got . . . problems.'

Beryl, ever eager for a gossip, lowered her voice. 'Oh. Anything I can do, love? Is it personal?'

Stella hesitated. 'Yes, Beryl, it is.'

'Well, I'm always here if you need—'

Stella interrupted her. 'Thanks, but I've got to go. I've got a lot to do.'

'Oh, you're not sick, are you? You sound different.'

'Beryl, I can't talk now.'

Stella put the phone down. On the floor where it had been thrown earlier was the photograph of her and Mike on their wedding day. She bent down and picked it up, using her apron to dust the glass, then carried it over to the sofa, the cushions still stacked up awaiting repair. Stella sat down and stared at the photograph, still in the silver frame they'd been given as a wedding present. She touched his face with the tips of her fingers, making a slow circular movement. Then she let the photograph fall to the floor. She remained sitting, staring ahead as, in slow motion, she saw herself as a young bride, her handsome Mike walking, floating down the aisle. She saw, as if it were only yesterday, the image of her father crying, big tears dripping down his face. It had been the proudest day of his life. Mike Hazard was the best rugby prop he had ever seen; he'd been a fan of his, watched him play. It had been her dad who had first introduced Stella to Mike. As she stood on the touchline one day with her father, he had said, his face aglow, 'Stella, if I'd had a son, I'd have wanted him like that lad. What an athlete! Look at the shoulders on him, he could turn professional. Look at the legs on him . . . look at him run!' He had always said that Stella's engagement to Mike, and then the wedding, was the proudest moment of his life. He said he felt happier that day than he had at his own wedding. Stella's mother had died when Stella was fifteen, so there was only her dad and a few of his relations who had flown over from Dublin for the wedding. They had continued the celebrations for the entire time Mike and Stella had been on honeymoon, and he had met them again on their return to Heathrow, well drunk, arms held wide – not for his daughter, but for his beloved Mike.

As Stella rose from the sofa she trod on the photograph, and the glass cracked beneath her foot.

She got into bed fully clothed, still with her apron on. There was no crying, just a terrible sense of loss. She felt as if she were dying: she ached, her heart hurt . . . the utter betrayal of everything she had valued and loved was slowly sinking in, becoming a reality. Somehow she knew Mike was never coming back to her. Even if he did turn up, she told herself, now he had a son, he had Susie, Susie was young, beautiful. Stella felt old. Used and abused.

Susie was still very drowsy. The comings and goings of the night staff kept waking her as they checked her pulse, and replaced the Elastoplast on her head. She had felt too weak to hold the baby, even when the midwife had told her it was a perfect little boy. She had a son. It seemed as if it was all happening to someone else. The pain had been real enough, the birth hideous – she had screamed herself hoarse. Now she just wanted to sleep, keep on sleeping. Nothing had really happened that day and that night, it was all just a nightmare. She would wake up in the morning and it would all have been a bad dream.

Midnight. A baby crying woke her. She was very confused and tried to sit up but her body felt stiff, alien. The baby cried on and off; she could hear footsteps, whispered voices, and then there was silence.

In the strange, small room she began to piece together each moment from the time Stella had walked into the office. Stella – Mike's wife. As the lies mounted up, Susie felt overwhelmed, unable to comprehend the web of deceit Mike had woven around her life. She had never really believed he was as bad as they made out – the accusations against him at the station, of bribes, of falsifying evidence over a period of many years – she had refused to believe them. She had known some were real, but there had been others involved, too, and she had gone along with Mike's anger, believed that he had been the 'fall guy'. Now she knew she had been wrong. He had lied so blatantly to her. Their entire marriage, their whole life together, had been founded on lies . . . She had never felt so dejected, so weak and helpless, so utterly alone. The sobs hurt, every intake of breath hurt. Her belly was still swollen, she ached so much physically – but that was easier than the mental anguish, that was the pain that hurt more than anything, and she couldn't stop the heavy, shaking sobs. At first she tried to muffle them, holding her hands over her mouth, but then she lay back and sobbed loudly, out of control.

The night nurse looked at her watch and got up from her little desk. She sighed. It often happened with the new mothers, the 'weepers' they nicknamed them, but this one, the black girl in the small private cubicle, was about to wake the entire ward.

'Can you see to the weeper in the end cubicle?' she asked her colleague. 'She's waking everybody up and you know if one starts they all have a howl!'

The young nurse nodded, but then the sound of Susie's sobbing stopped. They both listened. Everything was silent again, everyone was quiet, but as a precaution the young nurse walked quietly along the corridor to Susie's room, and eased open the door.

Susie was standing by the window, staring out into the dark night.

'You should be in bed, Mrs Hazard, you'll get cold.'

Susie turned, the girl stepped back. 'Get out. Just get out and leave me alone. *Out – get out!*'

'Can't you sleep?'

'I just want to be left alone. Now get out!'

The nurse shut the door, as the night sister looked up from

her desk, her face illuminated by the small Angle-poise lamp. 'Problem?'

'I don't think so. But she's up – and abusive. Told me to get out.'

The sister flicked through her reports, checking Susie Hazard's entry. She read it and looked up. 'She was the one brought in, emergency. Keep a check on her, maybe take the baby in to her.'

'We tried earlier, but she didn't want him near her.'

The sister sighed, looked back to the Susie Hazard entry, and noticed that she had had no visitors. No husband had been to see her, just her mother, a Mrs Stella Hazard.

CHAPTER FOUR

Inspector Levy walked out of the Richmond burns unit, and crossed to the doctor in charge of the patient. At least now they had a name for the man: James Donald. But that was about all they did have. He was still unable to be interviewed.

Detective Constable Kent was waiting in the car as Levy slammed the passenger door. 'We got an ID. His name's James Donald, but he can't talk. He's covered in bandages, they're doing a skin graft on his chest and hands. We'll run a check on him back at the station see if we got anything on him.'

Levy always felt as if Kent was breathing down his neck. A real high-flyer this one, Levy doubted he would stay local for long. He watched him working on the computer. That needled him, too; he'd never got the hang of the bloody things himself.

The fire experts' report had come in, and Levy read through their copious notes. The fire had been triggered off by a timing device, explosives, a bit obvious for an arson job. The head of the factory had been interviewed; he was devastated. If it was arson, would he be insured, was all he seemed concerned about. Not that two of his workers had died, and a third was seriously ill in the burns unit.

'James Donald!' Kent said as he laid out the computer print-out. 'He did work for Thompsons – but, guess what? He was sacked a year ago. He'd been doing some financial con with their own computers. He was a partner back in the early eighties, but then Thompson, the present owner, bought out the company. James Donald.'

Levy snatched the print-out. '*Oi*! I can bloody read, go and get me some tea and a bacon sandwich, I'm starving. Oh, and call the hospital, see when we can get in to Donald.'

Kent gave a tight-lipped nod. Levy liked to treat him as the office boy. Fetch this, do that – he could run rings round him. Maybe that was why.

'Anything on Hazard? The car, Gov?'

Levy pulled at his nose. 'Nope, but maybe he intended coming back for it and we got there first. Who knows? His domestic life isn't exactly ideal. If there's nothing on the cash, we'll release it.' Levy laughed.

Kent swung the door back and forth. 'What's so funny?'

Levy grinned. 'Well, if he was plannin' on doing a runner – gets a nice little hoard, maybe got another woman somewhere – he's gonna be well pissed off if we release the car and the dough back to his wife!'

Kent nodded. 'Yeah. She did seem pretty interested in how long it'd be before she could get her hands on it. You want sugar in your tea or have you got your sweeteners?'

Levy patted his pocket. 'Sugar. I've forgotten them again.'

Kent closed the door as Levy leaned back with his hands behind his head. It looked like they would clear up the arson case pretty quickly. Maybe he could get a round of golf in before he went home.

Alexander Reed was about to take his clubs out of his car when his portable rang. He reached into the car, then his face tightened. He looked around, not that any of the other golfers were interested. 'What do you want?'

Tony Laytham flicked the ash from his cigar. 'Is Hazard with you?' He listened, then covered the phone with his hand. 'He's not at Reed's place.' He returned to the call. 'He's got the disk, because Donald told me, and I don't think he was lying. What?'

Alexander Reed now sat inside the car.

'He called me, said he was worried about Donald, said he'd got cold feet . . .'

Reed listened, his face drained of colour. He licked his lips. 'Jesus Christ, there was no need to do that. My God, does Hazard know?'

Laytham ground out the cigar butt. 'No, we've not seen him, that's why I'm calling you. If he gets in touch, you contact me, OK? And, Mr Reed, don't try playing games with me. You understand what I'm saying? The disk is ready, we know for sure, so nobody is backing out, we keep things as arranged. Yes?'

Reed switched off the phone. His hands were shaking. It had already got out of control: he was caught. Now he was involved in murder and it scared the life out of him. The thought of playing a round of golf was suddenly the last thing he felt like doing. He needed a drink, a stiff one. He also had to get in touch with Hazard to try and control those two maniacs.

He dialled Hazard's office, waited as the answer machine bleeped on. He cut off the phone. His hands were clammy with sweat, and he jumped when his golfing partner banged on the side of the car.

Rodney Millbank, owner of the stud farm where Reed worked as trainer, smiled. 'You all set? We should get cracking, it looks like rain.'

Millbank walked away without waiting for an answer, pulling his golfing trolley behind him.

Millbank teed off first, then stood to one side as Reed took out his club. 'Everything going on course, is it? You seem a bit – frisky?'

The deep, plummy, confident tone of his voice got to Reed. 'Yes, it's all going as planned.'

Millbank watched as Reed swung his club. It was a good shot, and he cocked his head to one side. 'Well, whatever's bothering you hasn't put you off your stroke.'

Reed stashed his club, irritated that his nerves were showing. 'Just a bit under the weather, maybe a cold coming on.'

They began to walk across the green, Millbank wheeling his trolley, Reed carrying his set of clubs over his shoulder.

'Julianna was looking very good this morning! Wee Georgie

certainly knows his business. He was with me when I bought her, great jockey in his heyday, said he'd have given his right arm to race her, he's a good chap.'

Reed nodded, as Millbank's loud voice continued, 'I thought it would be rather a good idea to throw a bit of a party the night before the race, cover any comings and goings. The wife will organize the usual set. What do you think?'

Reed agreed, and totted up how many days before the race. Just a couple of weeks. He hoped to God there wasn't any further problem with Laytham. He'd try contacting Mike Hazard as soon as he returned to the stables.

Laytham replaced the phone. He'd got Hazard's answer phone again. 'What the hell you think he's playing at? I don't like this – it sucks.'

Kenny was tying and untying a piece of string. 'Well, maybe that fat slob Donald was lying. He said he give it to Hazard at the office, but it wasn't there, and it wasn't at the chick's place. He's a fuck-up, anyway. What's he doin' messin' around with two women?'

Laytham jabbed him. 'That was out of order. You shouldn't have slapped her around.'

Kenny shrugged. 'She caught me in the place. I didn't want her to see my face, did I? I reckon he's pulling one on us. I mean, where the hell is he? He an' that ponce Reed could be cutting us out. I warned you about Hazard. He's a sly two-faced bastard.'

Laytham stared, stuffing his hands in his pockets. 'We'll give it a couple of days.'

Kenny chucked his string aside. 'A couple? It fuckin' goes down in two weeks—'

Laytham whipped round. 'Eh! Watch who you're talkin' to – just zip it. We got two clear weeks, and now I got business, so get the car.'

Kenny glared. 'Yeah, yeah, but you remember if it wasn't for me you'd never have been able to use Donald.'

Laytham smiled and cuffed Kenny's face. 'I know, I know.

Now don't lose your rag. You can have some fun, on the house.'

Kenny grinned. His chipped teeth in his wide mouth made him look like a Hallowe'en turnip face. The girls all dreaded him, but if Laytham told them to be nice to Kenny they had no option. Suddenly Kenny was in a good mood, following Laytham down from the office area into the red wallpapered hallway. He carried Laytham's overcoat and black trilby. He didn't mind being his lackey; in fact, Laytham was the only person in Kenny's wretched life who had ever shown him any affection.

They had met in prison and he had been Laytham's lackey inside, too. For all Kenny's craziness, Laytham could control him, even if at times it felt as if he was a dangerous pitbull instead of a human being. Laytham knew how to muzzle him, and he kept him on a tight leash. He had seen Kenny when he had been let loose, and that side of him fascinated Laytham. It was a strange, powerful feeling to know you could say, 'Go, kill, Kenny.' And he would. He already had.

The two boys were messing around at the edge of the canal, just a few miles up from Mike Hazard's office. There had been heavy rain for days, and the water gushed over the weir. At first it looked like a sack of clothes as it slowly eased over the edge and flopped down into the water. The current carried it along the swollen banks: fallen branches, an old crate, thick black mud and slime covered what they had assumed to be a sack. Not until it floated right past them did they realize it was the body of a man. Bloated, his face distorted by the length of time he had been in the filthy water.

Mrs James Donald sat with Detective Inspector Levy. He asked about her husband and his connection with the Thompsons Computers factory. He wanted to know when she had last seen him and so forth. Mrs Donald was very nervous, constantly twisting her wedding ring round and round. She couldn't remember when she had last seen him but it was some considerable time.

Levy shifted his weight.

'I'm sorry, but that doesn't quite make sense to me. He's your husband? Yes? And you are not sure when you last saw him? But he did live here, yes?'

Mrs Donald nodded. 'But – we had this argument, oh, it'd be about two or three weeks ago and, well, he walked out.'

Levy nodded, looked to Kent who was busily making notes. 'We believe your husband was in a fire at – Mrs Donald?'

She stood up abruptly, almost in tears. 'I don't want to know what he's done. I just don't want to see him or ever speak to him again.'

Levy had pressed for more details, but Mrs Donald just started weeping. Even when he asked if she would accompany them to the hospital, she refused. She became almost hysterical, repeating 'I don't care! I don't want to speak to him, or ever see him again.'

Levy and Kent were on their way to the hospital when they received a call. A body had been found and taken to the morgue. Kent beamed: he'd really kicked up a storm at being sent to Richmond, now things looked like they were hotting up. 'Lot of action, Gov'. Arson. Now a possible murder!'

Levy shifted his weight in the car. 'It'll probably be some dosser that's fallen into the canal, so don't get your hopes up.'

There was no identification on the body. No wallet, nothing in any of the jacket pockets. In the top pocket of his suit, however, was a sodden card: Seekers Investigation Agency, and a blurred signature on the back of the card with Mike Hazard's name. This was the card Mike Hazard had given to James Donald to take to the garage, so his car would be fixed. Mike often scrawled his signature on the back of his agency cards as a form of 'pay you later'. The dead man was dark-haired, weighed about eleven stone, his height six foot two. There was no sign of violence on the body. He had drowned.

Due to the length of time he had been in the water, identification would be difficult.

Stella stood at the end of Susie's bed, carrying a bunch of flowers and a box of chocolates. Susie was sitting up. She smiled, 'I was hoping you'd come. Are you OK?'

Stella got a vase from the bedside cabinet. 'I'm as well as can be expected. How about you?'

Susie shrugged, plucking at the blanket. 'Have you heard from him?'

Stella shook her head. 'So you haven't either, then?'

Susie sighed as Stella rammed the flowers in the vase. Then she pushed the chocolates towards Susie. 'I can't stop, I've got to go to the shop. I work part time, and – they found his car. It was parked up by some factory that caught fire.'

Susie wanted to ask more about the car, if there had been anything in it, but Stella seemed edgy, embarrassed. 'I shouldn't have come, but I thought I'd better check that you were all right, and if there was anyone you wanted me to contact. Is there?'

Susie shook her head. There was so much they had to say to each other, but neither knew how to begin. Stella stood a moment, and then looked around the room. 'Where's the baby?'

Susie lay back into the pillows. 'He's in the nursery. They put them in there so we can have some sleep. It's a hell of a racket when they all start crying.'

'Well, I'd best be on my way. The manageress gets nasty, and I didn't go in for a couple of days. I've been clearing up the house.'

'Don't go yet, stay a bit longer. I mean, we should talk things through.'

Stella shook her head. 'There's nothing to talk about. How long will they keep you in?'

Susie shrugged again. 'I dunno, my blood count's a bit low or something. A few days, they don't keep you in long. He really hasn't called you?'

Stella pursed her lips. 'No. I went into the office, but there's

61

just some circulars, no real mail, and he's not been there.' She walked to the door. 'I'd best go. You take care.'

Susie was close to tears. 'Will you come again?'

Stella hesitated. 'No, I don't think so. Goodbye.'

Stella arrived at the Bake O Bread and was about to go in when she caught sight of Beryl's pink cap bobbing up and down as she talked to Maureen. She couldn't face them, so she returned home.

As she walked along the street, nearing her house, she saw that the young fresh-faced detective, the one that reminded her of a blond Clark Kent, Superman, was standing on her doorstep. He gave a small smile. 'Mrs Hazard. I . . . think we may have found your husband.'

Stella gripped the gate. 'Is that bastard at the hospital?'

Kent cleared his throat and said he was afraid it was bad news. He asked her if she would accompany him to the car, they wanted her to . . . His voice had trailed off. He'd never had to do this before, he was flushed with embarrassment. Levy got out of the car and looked at Kent. At last Kent had cocked up.

'Mrs Hazard, it's not very good news but we may be mistaken.'

He was interrupted as Stella turned to him. 'You've arrested him? Well, I wasn't – I mean, I wasn't going to press charges. I mean, she's had the baby, but the more I think about it . . .'

Levy took her arm. 'We've found a body. I'm sorry.'

Stella looked from one concerned face to the other. 'You think it's my husband? *Yes?* . . . Oh, God!' Somehow she kept on her feet, her breath coming in short, sharp gasps. Her pants and gasps became louder in the back of the car, and Levy turned to ask if she was all right. Stella nodded. She was trying every way she knew *not* to faint. Levy suggested that perhaps they could get someone else, another relative perhaps, but she shook her head: unable to speak, she couldn't tell him that there was no one else. She couldn't suggest Susie.

All afternoon she'd been working up such a hatred for

Mike, an anger she hadn't thought herself capable of feeling. Now she was dreading what was about to happen.

The clothes were shown to her first, still sodden. She touched them, then withdrew her hand quickly. It was then she was told that the victim had drowned. She panted a moment, unable to take it in. Mike was a strong swimmer, he couldn't have drowned, she told herself. They showed her the business card, Mike's name smudged on the back. Yes, it was his signature, blurred or not: he had very strong, bold writing, a big swirl on the 'd' at the end of Hazard.

They were very kind. A female plain-clothes officer was standing by as Levy quietly explained to Stella that the victim had been in the water for some considerable time . . . but that they would be right beside her.

'I don't know about the clothes. He had another woman, you see, two sets of clothes, so I can't be certain.' Just explaining it made her tense up, her hands clench.

Kent disappeared for a moment then returned, taking Levy aside to whisper that they had cleaned up the corpse and made it as presentable as they could to cause the least possible distress.

Stella turned to the policewoman, unable to stop talking. 'She's just had a baby, a boy, weighed eight and a half pounds. He had another woman and . . . that's why I can't be sure about the clothes. He must have had two sets, changed backwards and forwards. Hard to believe, isn't it?'

The female officer nodded, not at all sure what Stella was talking about, and she was rather difficult to understand as she kept gasping for breath, panting . . .

Levy touched Kent's arm. 'I'll take it from here.' He held Stella's elbow, a firm strong grip, as they entered the Chapel of Rest attached to the morgue.

The body was laid out, draped in a dark green sheet. Stella held back, and Levy didn't force her forward. He kept on talking quietly, explaining that she just had to take a look, he was right beside her, she had nothing to be afraid of – and, of course, there was always the chance that it was not her husband.

The green sheet was slowly lifted away from the head and shoulders by the attendant. Stella squeezed her eyes tight shut, and Levy asked if she was ready. One quick intake of breath and she opened her eyes to stare at the body . . .

The hair was dark, as dark as Mike's. It had been combed away from the forehead of the dead James Donald.

Stella blinked and was suddenly calm, incredibly calm. Had she wanted it to be Mike? What if it was Mike? Then it would all be over. It all came rushing into her mind: his life insurance policy, the house, the office, the money in the car . . . and she could just run away, like he had.

'Yes . . .' Her voice was hardly audible. 'Yes, yes, it's him.' She fainted then, collapsing into Levy's arms like a rag doll.

CHAPTER FIVE

James Donald's body was released for burial. The widow wanted him to be buried in the local church cemetery. The body could have been cremated, but there was a two-day waiting period and Stella had no time, she was moving like lightning . . .

The car and the contents of the black holdall were handed over to the widow. Stella asked the bank to send her all statements of their joint account, then she went to the insurance office. Mike Hazard's life was insured for one hundred thousand pounds. Stella had hardly slept as she attempted to get everything arranged as quickly as possible. She went to the local estate agents, and the terraced house was put on the market at a hundred and thirty thousand pounds. She went through Mike's desk and discovered that the office in the boatyard was on a ten-year lease. She returned to the estate agents and asked them to advertise the office premises, too.

Stella was never still, searching drawers for every document she might possibly need – old bank statements, the insurance policy . . . She was running against time. She feared Mike could turn up at any moment.

Stella arranged for the burial and the appointment with the life insurance brokers on the same morning. She felt dizzy most of the time: she hadn't been able to face food at all and she had lost nearly half a stone in weight. She felt almost drunk, running from one place to another. She called in at a travel agent's to collect an armful of brochures. She would, she had decided, go to the Costa Brava, buy a small apartment, and live the life she had always dreamed of. Not sailing into the sunset on the clapped-out old boat, but as a wealthy widow.

Stella dashed into the hairdresser's. 'Norma, I want a new look. Blonder. Can you make me blonder but still natural-looking?'

Norma, the fastest cutter and roller-up in the local salon, went straight for the Harmony Gold, and cut, restyled and blonded Stella in record time.

'Is it a party, Mrs Hazard?'

Stella admired the new look in the mirror of the salon. 'No, Norma, a new life . . .'

Stella ordered a firm of cleaners to go into the office. She wanted it stripped of all papers, everything thrown out, a splash of paint, and then it would be – as the estate agent had said – a possible but not an easy sale. She knew the house was on the market at a low price; again, the estate agent had said that even with the recession, at that price she could expect a quick sale.

Stella couldn't pass a dress shop without buying something. It was as though a madness had taken hold of her. Beryl had called but Stella told her that the manageress could stuff her job, she was never coming back, part time or any time.

'God almighty, Stella, what's happened? Last time I spoke to you, you sounded dreadful. What's going on?'

'New life, Beryl. I'm going to the Costa Brava.'

Stella could not bring herself to say or tell anyone that Mike was dead. It would almost make the fantasy bubble burst. The funeral was getting nearer and, armed with a large new leather bag filled with all the necessary papers, Stella drove to the local garage. She wanted the BMW sold. Her state of mind was obviously near breakdown level. The Costa Brava loomed – but the white convertible VW caught her eye. It was second-hand, immaculate, and only eight and half thousand pounds.

'I'll have that VW, the white – Golf, is it?'

The salesman couldn't believe his ears: she hadn't even sat in it.

'What will you give me for the BMW?'

He scuttled to the front garage display, about to insist she have a demonstration, but she interrupted and asked again, 'How much?' He replied that it would depend on how she wished to pay. He said they would give, maybe, fifteen hundred for the BMW, but they would require a banker's draft if she was paying by cheque.

'How much off for cash, then? I'll pay by cash.'

Stella drove off in the BMW, and returned half an hour later to hand over the money.

Stunned, never before having had such a customer, the salesman watched as she drove off the forecourt, almost ramming a bus in her eagerness to go.

Stella had her passport all ready and she was about to sort out flight tickets. She reckoned it would take a few days before they paid over the insurance money. The house and office sale could be completed without her being in England, as they could forward the money on to her.

She shot down the road in her new white convertible. She was already cutting it fine for the funeral, but she supposed she'd better change and wear a black coat to make it look good. She even ordered a wreath. 'Goodbye, Mike, I'll miss you . . .'

Stella charged up the path, scuffing her new high-heeled shoes as she kicked the front door open. She dashed up the stairs, and careered into the bedroom. Dizzy, she staggered to the bed and, as she flopped down, the bubble felt it was about to break. 'No, Stella, don't. Don't think about it, don't . . . Get your coat on!' But she had to lie down.

The enormity of what she had been doing over the past forty-eight hours suddenly hit her like a sledgehammer. She began her panting. 'Oh, God! Dear God, what have I done?'

She was terrified; she had committed a terrible crime, identified the wrong man, was now even about to bury him. The phone rang, and she cringed. What if it was Mike? She kept telling herself to let it ring, not to answer, but even as she said it she slowly slid off the bed, and went out onto the landing. As she looked down to the phone in the hallway, it seemed to have taken on a life of its own: ringing, ringing, ringing.

★

Susie stood at the payphone in the hospital corridor, waiting, waiting, and was just about to hang up when the small, frightened voice answered. 'Stella? Is that you? It's me, it's Susie.'

Stella had the telephone lead pulled to its fullest extension. She slumped onto the stairs. How could she tell her?

Susie felt wretched, but hearing the sad pitiful voice on the other end of the line seemed to make her feel stronger. 'It's all right, Stella. I know, I know about Mike. I've had one of the police officers here. They wanted to ask me about the night I was brought in, you know, the burglary and – Stella? Are you there?'

Stella licked her lips. 'Yes. Yes, I'm still here.'

Susie had to push in another fifty pence coin. 'Stella, he told me you're – that the body . . . Mike was released, and I'm sorry.' Susie couldn't stop the tears, she had to put the phone back on the hook. She knew she had no real rights, that she was not, after all, Mike's legitimate wife, but for Stella not even to tell her, not even to come and see her, made it so much worse.

Susie went back to her room, threw herself onto the bed, and sobbed. Mike was dead. No matter what he had done, it didn't matter now. He was dead. She reached over for a tissue, and blew her nose, loudly. She couldn't take it all in: when the officer told her that Mike had drowned, it didn't make any sense to her, but, then, nothing that had happened over the past few days made any sense.

The nurse came in carrying the baby. Susie hunched up on the bed. 'Go away. Just take him away, please. I can't deal with him. Just take him away.'

Doreen rocked the baby in her arms. 'Now, this has got to stop, Mrs Hazard. I know you're not breastfeeding him, but he needs body contact. You have to start to hold him. He's such a beautiful boy, such a good boy.'

Susie wanted to scream – she felt in more pain now than she had during the birth. Her body ached, her head throbbed, just seeing his tiny helpless face made her clench and unclench her hands. He was Mike's baby, his son, the child he had wanted, perhaps even more than she had. Now, with Mike dead, she had no one but that dependent tiny bundle and she was unable to feel any warmth or love. She wanted to be alone, she wanted to be held in Mike's arms, not be forced to hold the baby he would never see. Susie turned on Doreen, she flicked her hand towards the baby. 'I don't want him, *I don't want him!* I want – I want Mike! Oh, Mike. I want Mike.'

Doreen moved closer, her pretty round face full of concern. 'Is that the father? Is Mike his daddy, then?'

Susie looked at Doreen as if she was a moron. She snapped, '*Yes. Yes!*'

Doreen rested on the bed, still gently rocking the baby backwards and forwards. 'Well, why don't you let me call him? He'll want to see his baby, won't he?'

Susie bowed her head, feeling guilty about the way she had behaved towards everyone in the hospital. But how could they understand? 'Mike is dead. The baby's father is dead. Now, please, leave me alone.'

Doreen's china blue eyes filled with tears. 'Oh, I am sorry, so very sorry. I didn't know, none of us knew. Oh, Susie, I am so sorry.'

Doreen left with the baby, gently closing the door. Susie sat on the bed, no tears left, and she looked to a small stain on the wall. 'He's being buried this morning.' Susie repeated it to herself. Saying it aloud made it so final, and she faced the fact that it was true because, somehow, not until this moment had she really believed it. She stared around the horrible little room and reached out to ring the bell for the nurse. She kept her finger on the bell until she heard running footsteps, and then she released it and swung her legs off the bed.

Doreen was panting. 'Oh, I'd only just got to the end of the ward. I was telling Sister. She suggested that I ask you if you'd like someone to talk to you, to help you, *none of us knew*. Susie, would you like someone to come and talk with you? Help you over this crisis?'

69

Susie almost laughed. Crisis? Is that what she was going through? 'I need help, Doreen, but not that kind. I want to leave, and I also want to apologize to you – prove to you that I'm quite capable now. I'd like you to bring the baby to me, maybe stay with me for a little while.'

Doreen checked her watch and then looked towards the door. 'I don't think under the circumstances you should or could really leave just yet, but why don't you come and sit with the other mothers? Lunch will be served soon.'

Susie forced herself to smile. 'Lunch? Oh, well, why not? Can I get dressed?'

Doreen hesitated. She was worried about Susie – it was hard to believe she was the same person who, just a moment ago, had shouted at her but, then, new mothers often behaved irrationally. 'Perhaps you should just take it a stage at a time, Susie. I wouldn't get dressed, just wrap your dressing gown round you, and I'll help you down the ward.'

Susie sighed. 'I am not an invalid, Doreen, I just want to hold my baby and prove to you that I can take care of him. I want to go home. Is that too much to ask?'

Doreen did not stop Susie from dressing but kept a watchful eye on her until the next nurse came on duty. Susie had fed and changed the baby, had even chatted to some of the other mothers, but she began to tire during the latter part of the afternoon and returned to her room. When Doreen went off duty, Susie was sleeping, and the baby was in a crib next to the bed. Doreen had been on the maternity ward for years, but, as the day wore on, she became impressed with Susie's calmness. She seemed physically strong and, unlike many other women, didn't complain of pains or, after the initial flood of grief, break down in tears.

Susie wanted to leave as soon as possible, and was determined to do so. However, she knew that, after her initial outburst to Doreen, she would be under close supervision. She knew she had to prove beyond doubt that she was more than capable and felt fit. Apart from her still swollen abdomen, and the obvious discomfort, she was sure she could have walked out that afternoon. She still did not feel the mother bonding with her baby, but that didn't worry her. She had held him, had liked the warmth of his tiny body against her own . . . but he was part of Mike – and Mike was dead. She would have to provide for them both, and that was uppermost in her mind. Without Mike she was alone, and the baby did not ease, or help her come to terms with, her grief – or the betrayal. Mike had woven so many lies, and that was the biggest hurt, not the aftermath of childbirth. Nothing hurt as much as Mike's betrayal and his lies.

Levy slammed down the telephone and yelled at the top of his voice for Kent, who came rushing into the office. 'Car's waiting, Gov'.'

Levy lit his cigarette and inhaled deeply. 'Well, we don't need it, because—'

Kent moved closer. 'What's happened?'

Levy's face was almost hidden in a cloud of smoke. 'James Donald just fucking walked out of Richmond burns unit! Nobody knows where the hell he is.'

Kent pulled a face. 'Shit. Want me to—'

Levy jabbed the air with his finger. '*Find him!* That's what I want you to do. *Find him!*'

Al Franks was lifting his flask in a toast: 'Mike! Here's to you!'

Kenny Graham walked in and knocked the flask out of Al's hand. 'Where's Hazard? He been here yet?'

Al bent down for his flask – and got a kick in the face. He keeled backwards.

'Come on! Is he here? Have you seen him?' Kenny demanded, clenching his fists.

Al Franks could feel his nose blowing up. He touched it gingerly, then cringed back as Kenny moved closer.

'You deaf as well as stupid?'

Al shook his head. 'He's dead. Mike Hazard is dead. You wanna see him, he's being buried this morning. Now you get out or I'll call the cops.'

Kenny shot out, and the next moment Tony Laytham

walked in. He crossed to Al who sat dabbing at his nose with a handkerchief. 'Sorry about that idiot, mate. What's your name?'

Al muttered his name and that if that mad geezer showed his face again he would get the police on to him. Laytham opened his wallet. 'Look, forget him. He's – well, he's bit crazy, but, tell me, what's this about Mike Hazard?'

Al saw one fifty-pound note, then two, then three. At the fourth he told Laytham that Mike Hazard was dead; Mike's widow had told him. She'd been into the office earlier, and as far as he knew the funeral was some time this morning.

'How did he die?' Laytham asked, casually.

Al pocketed the cash fast, afraid it would be taken from him. 'I don't know, she never said, she was very upset . . .'

Laytham patted Al's shoulder, apologized again for Kenny's behaviour, then walked out.

Laytham got into the Mercedes. He sat a moment, drumming his fingers on the dashboard. 'Let's go see the widow. Drive around the cemeteries. That nose-on-legs in there said Hazard was being buried this morning, so let's make sure, OK?'

The Vicar had almost finished the burial – almost. Stella though he had and, desperate to keep her appointment with the insurance broker, she threw earth onto the coffin. The Vicar looked astonished. She bowed her head. 'Oh, I'm so sorry, I thought you'd finished . . .'

In a low monotone the Vicar continued, 'Ashes to ashes, dust to dust . . .' The gravediggers waited, spades at the ready, a respectful distance from the open grave.

Laytham and Kenny had been to three cemeteries before they located the right one. As Laytham leaned against the railings he could just see Stella, standing by the grave. There was no one else, and only one wreath.

Kenny moved close to Laytham. He asked softly, 'Is that the wife?'

Kenny stared. 'Yeah, that's her. She's the old one, the other one's black.'

Laytham and Kenny continued to watch. Laytham gripped Kenny's arm tightly to restrain him from confronting Stella as she hurried out of the cemetery.

'No, wait. Look at the gates, it's the filth.'

Levy and Kent drew up in the patrol car. Levy got out and hurried over towards Stella.

'I'm sorry, Mrs Hazard, we would have been here but, well, we've got a bit of an emergency on our hands. You have my sincere condolences.' Stella bowed her head meekly and thanked them both. As she said nothing else, they returned to their patrol car.

Stella walked on towards the white convertible, as Levy adjusted his driving mirror, watching her. 'She looks different. She look different to you?'

Kent turned and stared after Stella, watching her open the VW's driving door. 'No. Oh, yeah, maybe she's done something to her hair.'

They drove off, with Stella following them. Her heart was thumping – she had almost expected them to arrest her. She checked her watch: she was still on schedule, the meeting with Mr Sidgwick from the insurance brokers was not for another fifteen minutes.

Laytham watched Stella drive past. Almost to himself he said, 'She doesn't look like the grieving widow to me. Maybe you were right, maybe Hazard *is* pulling something on us.'

Laytham gestured for Kenny to follow Stella. Neither saw the figure step out from behind an old Victorian tombstone. The tall, well-built man moved uneasily, partly hidden between the stones. He stood by the fresh grave, then bent down and reached forward to look at the card attached to the wreath. His hands were encased in pink elastic protective burn covers. His hat hid the evidence that one side of his face was scarred; dark red inflamed scabs were weeping. The collar of his coat was turned up and had opened up the partly healed burns. He read the inscription and rose slowly, gazing at the fresh grave. He whistled softly, a strange, soft, low whistle, then looked over to the gates. In the distance he could see the vicar threading his way back to the chapel, talking to the gravediggers.

It was not until he started to walk that it became obvious that Mike Hazard was in considerable pain: a slow, shuffling walk. Twice he had to rest against one of the gravestones before he could continue on his way. The low whistle was replaced by a soft moan, his breathing thickened, he coughed – a rasping cough – and his hands in their pink bandages touched his chest. Each step seemed laboured. He wondered if he would be able to make it home.

CHAPTER SIX

Stella crossed and uncrossed her legs, her hands twisting the black leather gloves round and round. The sound of the clock ticking on Sidgwick's desk made her nervous. His balding head was bent forward as he sifted through the documents Stella had brought. The policy, the death certificate . . . He checked a large file at his elbow, then returned to flicking through the neatly pinned-together bank statements.

'Do you have the most recent statements, Mrs Hazard?'

'Pardon?'

Sidgwick tapped the bank statements. 'I will require notification from your bank, the most up to date—'

'Haven't I got it there?' Stella asked.

'No, these are . . . let's see . . . for the last quarter. You see, the life insurance policy is held against any debts that—'

'I don't understand . . .'

'Your husband used his life insurance policy as collateral, as well as the deeds of your house. I will also require—'

Stella stood up. 'I'll get them. What do they look like?'

Sidgwick explained that details of mortgage repayments, valuation of the property and so on would have been sent to Mr Hazard.

Stella interrupted him again. 'I know all the payments were made, the policy is up to date.'

Sidgwick nodded. According to the statements, that was correct. They had been paid by direct debit.

Stella leaned forward. 'The money is mine. As his widow I am entitled to . . .' She hesitated, realizing how mercenary she must sound or, if not that, desperate. 'I . . . you see, I have decided to leave Richmond. I want to go abroad, and I'd like everything settled. I can't stay here, not . . .'

She took out her handkerchief and blew her nose. Sidgwick hurried to her side. 'I understand. And I will make your case a priority. I am so sorry, this must be very distressing for you. If you would like, I can deal with the bank direct. I'll just need written confirmation that they can release all the necessary particulars.'

'But what has the bank got to do with his life insurance money?'

Sidgwick had already explained it to her once, but he repeated the position again. He spoke slowly, his voice soft, trying not to upset her. 'Any debts incurred by your late husband—'

'But he hasn't got any, and I paid in my own wages last week, and then, as you know, there was my father's legacy and—'

'Yes, yes. But this is really just a formality. I am sure everything is in order, but before I release any monies—'

She hurried to the door and he stopped in mid-sentence.

'I'll be back,' she said. 'I'll go to the bank now. What else was it you wanted? Oh, yes, the mortgage details.'

She was out and hurrying down the corridor. Sidgwick remained at the door. 'Mr Hazard will be sadly missed,' he called after her. Stella stopped and turned back to him. 'Yes, yes, he'll be missed. I won't be very long . . .'

Stella knew the papers weren't at the house, so she drove straight to the office. Her neck felt as if it was being squeezed. She twitched, her hands felt clammy on the steering wheel of the new car. She was in a desperate hurry to get into the office, terrified that the men she had ordered to clear up might inadvertently have thrown out the papers she needed.

Al Franks had wads of cotton wool stuck up both nostrils. Stella sped past him. 'Are they here? The men cleaning out the office?'

Al followed Stella to the stairs. 'Yes, and—' She didn't even wait to let him complete his sentence but ran up the small winding staircase. He could almost see up her skirt and couldn't help noticing once again that she had rather nice legs.

The two men were stuffing black bin liners with old files. As instructed they had brought paint and ladders to give the entire office a lick of paint. Buckets and cleaning detergents stood by ready to wipe down the paintwork. Stella burst in. 'Hold everything – I have to find some papers. Have you thrown any out yet?'

The men shook their heads, gesturing to the black bin liners. Stella tipped the contents out of one, searched through the old newspapers and magazines and picked up a file to flick through it.

Al Franks was on his cushioned easy chair, checking the racing news. Susie, with the baby in a carrycot, walked in. 'Seekers – office keys.' She didn't even say please. Al lowered the paper.

'It's open. They're painting it – er, wait, maybe I should take you up.'

Susie continued up the stairs. 'I know the way.'

'But Mrs Hazard—'

Susie whipped round. 'Yes! I am Mrs Hazard, all right?' Susie continued up the stairs, and then as she rounded the corner she had to put the carrycot down. She felt dizzy, her back ached, and she pressed herself against the wall. She took two or three deep breaths. Maybe she wasn't as fit or as capable as she had first thought. It was still very soon after the birth, and she was swamped by tiredness, weighed down by it. After a moment she felt better, refusing to give in to the exhaustion. Instead she kept telling herself she was not *like* all the others in the ward, the ones that kept on bursting into tears and complaining about being so tired they couldn't get out of the awful hospital beds. She was *different*. It was making herself feel angry that helped, and seeing the painters, seeing Stella really helped. She didn't have to think 'angry'. She was.

Al could feel his nose throbbing, so he sat back and picked up his paper again. Suddenly he decided he ought to make himself useful. If Mike's office was being stripped and sold he could be out of a job, so he went over to his broom closet. As he opened the doors his suitcase, packed with all his worldly possessions, tumbled out onto the floor. That was something else he needed to consider. He'd left his rented room, and had been dossing down in the cabin of the boat out in the yard. He had devised a plan to offer his services as night watchman free, if it was OK for him to kip out back just until he found alternative accommodation. He stuffed the case back into the closet, took out his brushes and was about to start making a show of cleaning the stairs when the sound of raised voices floated down the stairs. He hovered, making sure he got a good earful . . .

'You have no right to do this!' Susie shouted.

'I have every right. This is my husband's office, I am his widow and if I want it cleared out, I'll have it cleared out!' Stella shouted back.

Stella stood in front of Mike's desk. Susie was in the doorway. The two cleaners, like Al Franks, listened, fascinated, looking from one irate woman to the other.

Susie pushed her way in and placed the carrycot on the desk. Stella was flushed with nerves – seeing Susie had almost made her faint. 'You should be in hospital. Why aren't you still in hospital?'

'Because I discharged myself, and it looks like it was a good thing I did. Just what do you think you are doing?'

Stella folded her arms. 'I am having the place cleaned out and then I am selling it. There's ten years on the lease and there's nothing I want here.'

'You are doing *what*? Those files are all Mike's contacts.'

Stella pursed her lips. 'So what? I don't want them, the whole lot can go up in smoke for all I care.'

'Well, *I* care!' Susie retorted.

The two cleaners stood engrossed, like spectators at a tennis match, watching one woman then the other. Neither had the faintest idea of what was going on.

'My father's money bought this place, so I can do whatever I like!' Stella turned on the cleaners. 'Carry on! Go on, start chucking that lot out the back!' She pointed to the rubbish bags.

'You just stay put!' ordered Susie.

'*I* am paying them. You mind your own business.' Stella gestured for the men to carry on.

One picked up a bin liner and Susie snatched it away from him. 'Go and get a coffee or something. Go on, the pair of you!'

'Don't you move!' shouted Stella.

Susie almost pushed one man out of the door. 'Take a break, come back in fifteen minutes.'

Stella glared. Susie waved her hand for the second man to follow his mate. He looked at Stella. She sighed. 'OK. Go on, get some coffee.'

Stella followed them out into the corridor, and glimpsed Al's unmistakable red nose peering up from the staircase. 'Are you enjoying yourself? Get back to your work, go on!'

Al shot back down, as the cleaners headed for the stairs. They were slightly nonplussed by all the drama, but not unduly concerned – they'd been paid upfront for the job, so it didn't bother them.

Susie slammed the office door, and confronted Stella. 'Right. Let's talk this through.'

'No, there's nothing to talk through. I'm leaving. I'm going to the Costa Brava and nothing you say—' Stella stopped in mid-flow as the baby started to cry. Susie jiggled the cot with her hand, but he continued. She shoved at the cot a bit harder. 'Don't do that!' Stella said, and she bent over the carrycot. Susie threw up her hands in frustration. Trying to get any sense out of Stella was like talking to a wasp: her mind flitted and zipped from one subject to another. 'He needs changing. Have you got a clean nappy?'

Susie wrenched open her large bag, and took out a box. 'I'm going to have to get a job, Stella. Now – are you listening to me? Yes? I've thought about it, and I reckon I can take over this agency and—'

Stella rocked the baby in her arms. 'That's not really my business. Like I said, I have my own plans. I've got a lot to do and . . .'

Susie laid out the nappy on the desk and held out her arms for the baby.

Stella peered at the nappy. 'It's inside out. You don't put the plastic side to his skin! Turn it over.'

Susie banged the nappy round the correct way. Stella gently undressed the baby and laid him down, as Susie paced around the office.

'Look, Stella, can you concentrate for a second? Whatever money you put in, we'll have to sort that out, but I also put all *my* savings into this business. We were going to be partners, Mike and me, that was what we had arranged, soon as the baby was born. And – Stella, are you listening to me? I need this business. Stella?'

Stella wrapped the nappy round the baby, and handed him back to Susie, who began to dress him again. He was quiet now as she pulled up his white Babygro, then wrapped the blanket around him before slipping him back into the carrycot.

Stella had to turn away. The baby seemed to have sapped the anger out of her. Susie tucked the child's blanket around him. She was still furious. 'You didn't even let me know about the funeral. How could you do that? You know how I found out Mike was dead? The police told me. They wanted me to complete a report about the break-in, and "Oh! yeah! your husband is dead. We released his body to his widow . . ." Can you imagine what that did to me? You never even told me. How – how could you do that?'

Stella looked at her watch. She still had to find the papers and get back to Sidgwick. Her face was flushed with guilt. 'I don't really want to talk about it. I just think you should go. If you want the files, then take them – take anything you want.'

'I want the office. I can't work from the flat.'

Stella's neck was tightening again. She twitched. 'I'm selling everything, but—' She picked up her handbag. Turning away from Susie she took out a bundle of notes. 'Here. This will tide you over.'

Susie looked at the money. 'Tide me over? Didn't you hear

me? I said that my savings went into this business, and I have no intention of—'

Stella butted in, unable to face any more. 'Right now, all I am concerned with is *my* life, not yours. I don't want anything to do with you, and under the circumstances—'

'I'm calling him Mike.'

'Pardon?'

'I said, I am calling the baby Mike.'

Stella had to give a few quick pants. 'Fine. Now, please, I'd like you to leave. I have an appointment.'

The baby started to whimper. Susie looked at her watch. 'Oh, God, it's time for his feed.' She searched in her bag, close to tears. 'Damn it, I've left his bottle in the car.'

She walked to the door, Stella following. 'Where are you going? Aren't you taking the baby?'

Susie opened the door. 'I'm just going to get his bottle. I'm not through yet, Stella, we really need to talk this over.'

'There's nothing more to be said.'

Susie's face was expressionless, but there was a hardness to her. 'Yes, there is. I won't be long. I've had to park over the bridge, somebody's already in the bay.'

'I am. That's my car.'

Susie stared at her. 'Yours? That white convertible is *yours*?'

Susie suddenly took a closer look at Stella: she was flushed bright pink, her head twitching. Only now did Susie notice the new hair-style, the high heels . . . and the expensive two-piece suit. Susie looked her up and down, and then gave a strange sidelong glance. Something didn't feel quite right.

'I'll get the bottle. Like I said, we've got to talk.'

Al Franks started dusting frantically as Susie walked past him. Outside, the two cleaners were lounging around. Susie paused. 'Have you been paid? Yes? Well, this is your lucky day! You can go. Come back for your ladders later.'

Stella searched through the filing cabinets. The baby whimpered, and she went over to his carrycot. In contrast to Susie, she rocked the cot gently, made soft 'shushing' sounds. She heard the office door open behind her, expecting it to be Susie returning.

'He's got a lot of hair. Will it fall out? New babies often have a lot of hair, but then they lose it.'

Stella's own hair – her whole head – was yanked backwards.

Tony Laytham pushed her roughly to one side. She stumbled, terrified. 'What – what do you want? Who are you?'

'Mrs Hazard?'

Stella nodded, rubbing her head.

'I'm a friend of your husband. He had something that belonged to me. A disk, a computer disk.'

Stella stared, then swallowed. Laytham stepped closer, and his eyes were hard, dark, close set; frightening, unfeeling eyes. 'The disk is about so big.' He gestured with his hands.

'I don't understand!' Stella gasped out.

Laytham sighed. 'I don't want to hurt you, or . . .' He placed his hand on the carrycot. 'I want the disk. So you find it, OK? You got twenty-four hours, and don't . . . don't go to the cops, don't do anything silly, because I know Mike had it – and I know where you are. I'm watching every move you make. I'll be back.'

Laytham left as quietly as he had entered. Panting, Stella stumbled over to sit on Mike's chair. She put her head between her legs, feeling dizzy, it ached where Laytham had almost torn out her hair from the roots.

Al Franks was out in the boat. He stashed away his suitcase, then opened his sleeping bag. It wasn't much, but at least it was dry and he could sleep in peace. Perhaps he wouldn't even mention it to Mrs Hazard: nobody would know he was there. Al hadn't seen Laytham enter or leave. Neither had Susie.

Stella watched as Susie gave the baby his bottle, uncertain whether or not to tell her about the visit from the awful man. She was twitching again as she kept on thinking about what she had done, telling herself she was out of her mind to have gone this far. She was on the verge of blurting everything out, confessing the whole truth to Susie because she was so scared. And then, any minute, Mike could walk back in, any moment it might all come out anyway. The tears started.

Susie, busy concentrating on the baby, hadn't even noticed. The baby was refusing his feed. Irritated, she shook the bottle. Stella sniffed and Susie became suddenly aware that she was upset, but she chose to ignore it. Instead she shook the bottle again furiously, examined the teat, squirted a drop on her hand, as Stella watched.

'You should wind him. That young he can't—' Stella sniffed again, wiped her cheeks with the back of her hand, 'he can't digest properly. Just pat his back, make him burp. It'll be wind making him miserable – here, I'll do it.'

Stella took the baby, and rested him against her, gently patting his back. She felt the bottle, it was lukewarm: at least Susie had got that right. 'Did you have a special container to keep it warm?'

Susie didn't reply, she was looking through the files. 'Did Mike have a life insurance policy?'

'Pardon?' The baby sucked at the bottle.

'I said, or I asked, if Mike had an insurance policy.'

Stella watched the baby turn his head, refusing the bottle. He'd had enough, so she burped him again. Susie repeated her question.

The baby gave another gurgled burp. Stella laid him back carefully in his carrycot. Susie watched her slow, deliberate movements: Stella was the most infuriating woman she had ever met.

'I know he had a life insurance policy, Stella. I was just wondering how much it was for? I mean, if you have that, it seems only fair that I should retain the office and—'

Stella took a deep breath. This was ridiculous, she couldn't go on like this. Then Susie held up a thick set of papers. 'You selling the house? You'll need these, they're the mortgage payments from your bank.'

Stella snatched them out of her hand. 'Thank you. And –

yes, Mike did have an insurance policy but the amount is my business.'

Susie pushed at Stella. 'This agency is *my* business. After all, my money went into it.'

Stella suddenly hated Susie; she was arrogant, over-confident. If Mike walked back in right now – so what! Suddenly she was fighting mad again.

'When I sell – and not until I sell – you'll get a cut. Until then, I'd like you to leave.'

'Did they find his car?' Susie, hands on hips, demanded an answer.

Stella faced her and looked straight into her glaring, angry face. 'I don't know. And now I have an appointment, so would you mind leaving?'

Susie walked to the desk, casting an eye around the office. She picked up the carrycot. 'I mind, but I'll go and I'll call you later. I'm going to see a lawyer, you have no right to—'

Stella said sharply, 'I have every right to do what I like! I am Mike's legitimate wife. You, in case you are not aware of it, have no rights to anything.'

Susie carried the baby to the door, not even turning back. 'We'll see about that. I'll fight you, Stella. I have Mike's son, and I won't give up this agency because it's going to be my future as well as his!'

She flung the door closed behind her with such force that it shook. Stella's legs buckled and she slumped into the chair. At least Mike hadn't walked in. Maybe there was still time, maybe she would be able to do what she intended. But right now she felt at a loss, wanting to cry, needing someone to help her. She was scared, even momentarily forgotten the man who had pushed her around. She was getting more and more confused by the minute. Who on earth could she turn to? The terrible feeling of desolation swamped her again. She had never done anything against the law in her entire life. But now? Everything seemed to be growing darker by the second. Remembering what she had done – burying a man she didn't know – and now making a false claim on Mike's life insurance, the thought frightened her. She could go to jail!

*

Stella left the mortgage documents with Sidgwick's secretary, together with a note giving him authority to contact her bank.

She had talked herself back into some semblance of control. She was going to go home and pack. If the money was released, as she hoped, within twenty-four hours, she would be on her way. Susie, she had decided, could bloody well keep the office. She'd been stupid about standing in her way, it was just some kind of revenge on her part. Mike would come back and the two of them could run the agency, could do what the hell they liked. But one thing Stella was damned sure of: they wouldn't have a penny that rightfully belonged to her. She'd make them both pay for the hurt she suffered. And it *was* hurting; even in her new car, with her new hair-style and new clothes, she couldn't stop the pain gnawing inside her, a constant dull ache. She talked and talked to herself, forcing herself to keep under control – and to move as fast as possible before Mike made an appearance.

Inspector Levy left James Donald's house. Mrs Donald had been as nervous as on his previous visit, but this time they had arrived with a search warrant. Donald was not on the premises. He seemed to have disappeared off the face of the earth. Hospitals, local doctors and clinics had been alerted to contact the police if anyone suffering serious burns approached them for treatment. Levy doubted if Donald could stay at large for long; his injuries were extensive, and would, according to the doctor who had treated him, require constant cleaning and medication. He was astonished that he had been able to walk out of the hospital.

Mike Hazard, nervous of being noticed on buses or any public transport, had made the slow, long painful walk back to his home. Only after a few stiff drinks did he feel able to make it up the stairs to the bathroom. The burns to his face were weeping badly. He dabbed them with iodine which stung so much that he gasped out loud. The chest bandages were stiff with pus and blood. He gingerly inched them away, and poured the iodine over his chest. Once again he moaned. He ripped a sheet into shreds and made pads, soaked in iodine, to rest against the wounds. Then he wrapped the torn sheet around his body.

He could feel his strength draining from him and had to grip the sides of the washbasin tightly to steady himself. Gritting his teeth, he breathed deeply through his nose. He was going to have to face Stella, find out what she thought she was doing – and who, in God's name, she had buried.

Slowly Mike made his way into the bedroom. He found a suitcase and dragged a few clothes into it. It was then that he saw the holdall, the one from his car. He couldn't believe it, and gave a great sigh of relief when he saw the bundles of notes. Painfully, he stood up and only just managed to make it to the bed. Exhausted, racked by pain, he carefully lowered himself down and lay there, trying to think what in God's name had happened. It was all a terrible mess, everything that had seemed so simple on the surface had spiralled out of control. But what confused him most were Stella's actions – and the funeral.

Beryl poured Stella a cup of tea. She'd remarked on the new hair-style, had seen her drive up in the white convertible. Beryl couldn't help but wonder; she knew the 'merry widow' syndrome – but, well, Stella had only buried her husband that morning . . .

Stella didn't really know why she had stopped by, she just needed to talk to someone. She was even considering telling Beryl the terrible thing she had done. Her hands twisted a small scrap of tissue round and round.

Beryl spooned in the sugar. 'You should have told me 'bout the funeral – none of us at the shop knew.'

Stella sipped the hot sweet tea. Beryl's kids were playing a video game in the other room, the pings and whizzes a constant background noise.

'You left all right then, are you? Financially secure, yes? I saw the new car – very nice. When my bugger walked out –

not that it's the same as dying, but, by Christ, I've wished him dead. Do you know, he'd been going around with another woman for years, and I'd been paying for her? He could never hold a job down for more'n a few months . . .'

Stella licked her lips. 'How did you feel when you found out?'

Beryl snorted. 'If he'd come anywhere near me I'd have cut his pecker off with a carving knife! I was left destitute, *destitute* – and her! The one he left me for was half his age, the soft git. Well, I heard she'd dumped him. He went back to Ireland – Irish, see, never trust them . . .'

Beryl suddenly realized Stella was Irish.

'Just the men, I mean, the women are all right – it's Irish men. The yarns that bugger spun me! And all the time, do you know he'd even – even had her here in his own house, in my bed! I know that for a fact because I found an earring.'

Stella now knew why the manageress of the Bake O Bread had warned her never to discuss Beryl's missing husband. Beryl didn't draw breath for a good hour, but in some ways it helped. Stella didn't really listen, and only came to when Beryl offered her a cigarette for the third time.

'I said, what'll you do now?'

Stella lit the cigarette and slowly inhaled, letting the smoke drift through her nose. 'I'm going to the Costa Brava.'

Beryl sighed. 'Oh, you lucky woman. I've dreamed of moving some place where there's sun, and beaches and . . . a handsome, tanned hunk. God! What I wouldn't give for a tanned body-builder. It's been my fantasy, you know, but well, this is where you're lucky – you've not got anything to keep you here, no kids . . .'

Stella nodded. 'Yes, that's right, I've nothing to keep me here – and if I find a bronzed god I'll send you a postcard!'

That same night, Kenny eased back the earth. It hadn't been as hard as he'd thought, it was so fresh, but it had still taken him over an hour. Laytham had remained sitting in the car, waiting. He had been reading the local *Kingston Free Gazette* newspaper. He stared at page three, and then looked back to the gravestones. In the darkness he could hardly see Kenny. He had a good idea who was in that grave.

The coffin was secured shut, and Kenny used a screwdriver to prise open the lid. The stench made him vomit . . .

Laytham saw Kenny stamp down the earth, then walk towards the car. If anyone had appeared, Laytham would simply have driven off, but there hadn't been even one solitary passer-by.

Kenny was filthy, his face covered in streaks of muddy soil, his hands and shoes caked in it. He climbed into the car.

Laytham looked at him. 'Well?'

Kenny wiped his face. 'The stench made me throw up all over the bleedin' coffin.'

'It wasn't Hazard, was it?'

Kenny shook his head. 'It was James Donald. I had to push his face about to be really sure . . .'

Laytham cringed away from Kenny, as he elaborated details of the decomposing corpse, then he passed over the newspaper, folded at page three.

'I guessed as much. Read that. The cops are looking for him, reckon he started that blaze at the factory.'

Kenny read the paper as Laytham drove the car. 'Says here he was taken to Richmond hospital, but he couldn't have been, I mean, he was already dead, wasn't he?'

Laytham gave a sidelong glance at Kenny. 'You thick shit, of course it wasn't him in the fire. Who the hell do you think it was? What did Donald say? He was gonna go to the factory with Hazard, only . . .'

Kenny flapped the paper down on his knee. 'It was Hazard. He was in the fire, yeah?'

Laytham flicked on the radio. 'That's right, Kenny. All ticking over, is it?'

Kenny nodded. 'So what's next? We go to the hospital or what?'

Laytham sighed. 'You've just read, Kenny, that the cops are looking for a man they presume is Donald, because he walked out of the friggin' hospital. You know – *I* know – it wasn't James Donald, it was Hazard in the fire. His wife went through that charade burying him, so his wife's got to be in the know. He's trying it on.'

Kenny's mouth dropped open; he couldn't get it together. Laytham slammed on the brakes in frustration. 'Donald told us he'd given Hazard the disk! The fucker's got it – and he's cutting me out, he's cutting you out! *Sunk in yet? Got it yet?*'

Kenny nodded dumbly, and Laytham drove on.

'So where we goin' now?'

Laytham said nothing as he paused at a set of traffic lights.

'I said, where are we goin' now?' Kenny repeated.

Laytham turned. In the yellow glare of the traffic lights his face looked eerie. 'Where's he gonna hide? With the black cow or the old bitch? One or the other, so we wait . . . We'll find him.' Laytham suddenly gave a short, shrill shriek: he was laughing. 'He's a dead man anyway, isn't he?'

The house seemed to be in darkness, but when Kenny crouched down and peered through the letterbox he could see there was a light on in one of the rooms upstairs in the house. He returned to the car, and leaned in. 'Somebody's in there – well, there's a light on, and guess what?' He grinned.

Hazard had been in such a state when he arrived earlier that for a moment he'd even thought Stella had changed the locks, but then he'd pushed at the door and had hurt his hands so much he had forgotten to take the key out. It was still there.

Looking down from the bathroom window Mike could see the two men outside, and swore at his own stupidity. He saw Kenny moving back up the pathway. Mike wanted to write a message; he knew the time had come when he needed Stella's help. He made his way back into the bathroom.

Kenny checked out the sitting room, then thudded up the stairs. He was half-way up when Mike Hazard walked out of the bathroom.

89

'Well, well, well. You and the wife are quite a team!' Kenny's cracked smile was crazier than ever. 'I just puked all over that fat slob Donald's face.'

Mike bent down and picked up the holdall. 'I need a doctor.'

Kenny giggled. 'That's an understatement. When I finish with you, you're gonna be on a slab in the morgue! We want that disk, we know you've got it.'

Mike walked step by step down the stairs, using the rail to help himself down. 'I don't have it.'

Kenny kicked out and Mike fell face forward. He screamed in agony.

'I gave that black tart the same treatment, but she still had yer kid . . . you know? You got a bastard kid.' Kenny kicked Hazard, and he curled up to protect his chest, but his hands were useless and he couldn't even try to defend himself. Kenny was about to put the proverbial boot in again when Hazard rolled aside.

Tired of waiting, Laytham walked in the front door just in time to see Kenny swing another vicious kick at Hazard. 'That's enough! *Kenny!*'

Laytham crossed to Mike, bent down, and rested back on his haunches. 'We want the disk, Mike. If we don't get it, your kid won't see his first birthday. Now, if that's the way you want to play it, you know how Kenny likes a game of football – and with you being a dead man, nobody's gonna do nothin', nobody will even look for you. We can put you in the grave with your pal Donald. It's up to you . . .'

Mike eased up, pushing with his feet so that he could rest against the wall. 'I need a doctor, I need someone to fix my chest. I don't have the disk but I know where it is. You'll have it on condition you get me out of here. So tell that crazy motherfucker to back off me, or you'll get fuck all!'

Kenny was about to kick out at Hazard yet again when Laytham pushed him aside. He gave Mike an outstretched hand to assist him to his feet. He noted the strange pink encased hands and could see the pain Hazard was in: he looked a complete mess, his face scarred and blistered.

'You shouldn't have tried this on me, Mike, not on me.'

Laytham put an arm around Mike's shoulder. Mike winced. 'I never tried anything. You think I'd get myself burnt up like this on purpose? What do you think I am? Crazy as Kenny?'

Laytham withdrew his arm as Kenny tried to punch Mike. 'That's enough! So, what you sayin', Mike? Huh?'

Mike saw Kenny checking over his holdall. 'I'm saying, get me a doctor, get me hidden, and it'll all go through just as planned.'

Laytham nodded, as if agreeing.

Kenny displayed the holdall. 'It's his cash, some gear, a suit – but a lot of dough.'

Mike looked to Laytham, knew that Kenny was his dumb yes-man. 'For Chrissakes, get me out of here.'

'Where's the disk?' asked Laytham, not trusting Mike. Kenny was checking over the cash.

Mike gave a lopsided smile. 'You'll get it in good time. First, get me out – before I really am a dead man.'

Laytham took the holdall, and ordered Kenny to assist Mike to the car. The front door was shut. Kenny giggled as he held up the key, but pocketed it when Mike reached out for it. 'Nah! Just in case I need to come back . . .'

They had to help Mike into the back seat. He was half in and half out of the car when Stella, driving the VW, turned into the street.

Kenny slammed the rear door and Laytham was already starting the engine as Kenny ran round to jump into the passenger seat.

Stella only half saw the Mercedes moving off; she was concentrating more on looking for a parking space. She took her time reversing in and out, in and out. By the time she was parked, the Mercedes was out of sight.

Mike leaned back, his eyes shut. He felt as if his whole body was on fire. Just the shuddering of the car's engine hurt him. Every time they turned a corner and his body shifted position he grimaced with pain. 'What was that about a baby?'

Kenny turned round. 'That cow. She was screaming the place down, she freaked me out . . . So . . . well, I give her a bit of a tap.'

Mike kept his eyes closed, showing no reaction. Laytham watched him in the driving mirror. 'You know the way Kenny gets. He didn't hurt her too bad, though, did you, Kenny? Baby was in the office, we been there today, so no harm done? Eh?'

They drove on, Laytham repeating his words, 'I said, Mike, no harm done?'

Mike's voice was hardly audible. 'No. No harm done.'

Laytham continued driving for a while in silence. 'I'll take you to the Rosemount, you'll be safe in there. Get somebody to take a look at you.'

Mike muttered his thanks. Laytham passed over Chiswick Bridge. 'I want that disk, Mike. You mess me around, like I said, you are a dead man. Knockin' you off isn't gonna be a problem, so let's be straight with one another, OK? And you don't want Kenny beatin' up on that wife of yours again, now, do you?'

'No, no, I don't.' Mike was leaning back against the seat, his eyes closed.

Kenny giggled. 'Oi! What's with you havin' two, then? I mean one's bad enough, what you want two for? Mike? Eh! Mike?'

Again, Laytham watched Mike's reaction in the driving mirror. Kenny leaned over and pushed at Mike. 'I think he's passed out . . .'

Laytham gave a strange high-pitched screech of a laugh. 'Just so long as he's not died on us!'

'Nah!' said Kenny. 'He's passed out, he's still alive.'

You won't be, Kenny, not for long, Mike thought, as he half opened his eyes to look at them – Kenny's big muscular frame, Laytham's neat, dapper shoulders. Mike knew he had to get his strength back first. Then he'd kill Kenny, maybe kill them both. He was in agonizing pain, but what hurt him just as much was the fact that his child had been born, he didn't even know if it was a boy or a girl – and the madman sitting in the front seat, crazy Kenny with his chipped teeth, had beaten Susie up . . . Thinking of her made him want to weep. What a mess he had made of everything. Poor Susie . . . he'd make it up to her, make it up to his – did he have a son or a daughter?

'Was it a boy?' Mike asked softly.

Kenny turned back. Laytham asked what Mike had said, but Kenny shrugged. 'I think he just moaned.'

Mike never gave a thought to Stella, the hurt he had inflicted on her or his betrayal. He could only think of his beautiful Susie, and his child. He hoped it was a boy.

Stella didn't feel hungry, her head throbbed. It had been difficult to get away from Beryl and she wished she'd never called round to see her. Too tired to pack her suitcases, she decided she'd do it tomorrow. She caught sight of the bedroom light and froze. She knew she had turned it off, knew instinctively that someone had been, or perhaps still was, in the house..

'Mike? Mike?'

Stella inched open the door of the bathroom. At first she thought it was blood. The iodine stains were on the bathmat, the floor and the walls, it dripped down the sides of the washbasin. She was going to scream – but then she saw the stained, blood-soaked bandages.

'Mike?' The panic rose, she couldn't get her breath, she panted, panted . . .

Then she saw something was scrawled in dark brown iodine on the bathroom mirror.

'Disk, bottom of F cabinet Offic' The last word had not been completed, and the message made no sense to her. It was all so horrible. Stella stumbled back out of the bathroom and into the bedroom.

The wardrobe door was ajar, the bedcover askew. It was obvious that someone had been there, that someone had lain on the bed. She checked the wardrobe. Clothes gone, shirts, a suit. She bent down and dragged out the shoes . . . but she

93

knew it would have been taken. She was right. The holdall, with all the cash from Mike's car, had gone.

Stella hit out at the wardrobe door with her fist. She shouted at the top of her voice. She had never in her entire life felt such blazing rage. She screamed . . . *'You bastard! You Bastard!'*

CHAPTER SEVEN

Stella hadn't slept a wink – tossing and turning, getting up and making a cup of tea. Pacing the bedroom, she checked and double-checked that the money and the holdall had really gone, half believing she had been mistaken. But she hadn't. Just for something to occupy her, she started to wash down the bathroom, remove the iodine stains – anything to keep herself busy as she grew more and more frightened. The strange message scrawled on the cabinet mirror still made no sense to her. She reckoned that by now Susie would know everything: she would know what she had done. Mike must be in some kind of trouble; those awful men, the house being ransacked. Well, it wasn't her problem any more. Susie was welcome to him.

When the doorbell rang, Stella's heart thudded. What if it was the police? Would they arrest her for allowing that man to be buried? Would they have found out by now that she had tried to claim on Mike's life insurance policy?

'Stella? It's me! It's Susie! Can you let me in?'

Susie stood on the doorstep, loaded down with two suitcases, and various carrier bags.

'I'm sorry to do this to you, Stella, but this morning the bailiffs arrived.'

Stella looked at all the luggage. 'Where? At the office?' She checked her watch. 'But it's only eight thirty.' Her heart thumped. 'Is Mike with you?'

'Yes. I'll go and fetch him.'

Stella had to lean against the hallstand for support. Oh, God, she was going to have to face him.

Susie locked up the car, and carried in the carrycot. Stella suddenly realized Susie was referring to the baby, not to big Mike.

'Are you going away, then?' Stella started to feel calmer.

'No. I was wondering if, well, if I could stay a few days until I get a place sorted . . .'

'Stay? You want to stay here, in the house, with me?' Her panic surged back into life again.

Susie took the baby out of his carrycot. 'Yes, I'm sorry. I know you're going abroad, I know it'll be inconvenient but—'

'You want to stay here with me?' Stella repeated.

Susie tucked into eggs and bacon. Stella held the baby and his bottle on her knee. Susie had made no mention of Mike. All she talked about was how the bailiffs had arrived, and how no amount of arguing or cajoling, showing them the baby, explaining that she had recently been widowed, made them reconsider. The owner of the property had turned up and accused her of squatting. He asserted he had not seen a penny since the day he had rented the flat to Mike Hazard, and he had given more than adequate warnings over the past six weeks that they would be evicted. Now he was past taking notice of any excuses – no babies, nothing.

Susie had a streak of butter across her cheek. She ate like a small child, ravenous, shovelling in the food at an alarming rate. 'He'd never paid the rent! There's electricity and gas bills outstanding and – I couldn't believe it! Could I have another cup of tea?'

She watched as Stella deftly juggled baby and teapot. Then Stella glanced up catching Susie's look. 'I had all these maternity classes when I was expecting. We had a life-size doll we used to practise on. I used to go with a friend of mine, she was near eight and a half months, I was just a few months, but we went together. I thought it'd all be good practice – and she was ever so ill, sick! So I went with her back and forth and got a bit of practice in at the same time. Funny how life works out. She got twins and I got nothing, lost it at six

96

months, but I know at his age, being so young, you've always got to keep his head steady. He needs changing, too. Did you bring his clean nappies?'

Susie was installed in the spare room, and the baby could sleep either with her or in the small boxroom. He was washed and changed, fed and burped: Stella issued instructions to Susie to bring the washing-up bowl from the kitchen. She cleaned it and balanced it on a wide board across the bath. She had searched out all her baby books, then taken out the baby clothes she had amassed in a drawer during the time she hadn't been able to resist the temptation to buy. They were horrid little teddy-bear suits, complete with ears and padded feet. Susie roared with laughter, telling Stella that she couldn't possibly put Mike in them, but Stella retorted that they were warm – and, besides, carting a newborn baby around in just a carrycot was not a good idea. 'You've always got to keep his extremities warm – it's in all the books.'

Mike, duly encased in his blue teddy-bear rig-out, was stashed back in his cot. Stella had hardly had time to run a comb through her hair. She noticed that Susie had left the breakfast dishes on the table, in fact had just shifted them aside as she sat in her raincoat waiting for Stella.

Susie was getting irritated, but trying hard not to show it. Stella had still not agreed to her taking over the agency and was not sure where the lease documents relating to the office were. Obviously, if Susie was going to take it over, they'd be vital.

'Why don't I just meet you at the office, Stella?'

She had been waiting at the foot of the stairs for five minutes. Stella appeared at the top. 'No, we'll go together – I'm just making the beds.'

'*Leave* the beds, Stella, we'll do it when we get back!'

Stella pursed her lips. 'It's done, I'm ready now – just give me two minutes.'

Stella didn't want Susie out of her sight: this way, if Mike tried to contact her or call her at the office, she'd be able to intercept the call.

*

Al Franks came to the main doors of the boatyard just as Stella drove in, followed by Susie. They parked side by side. Al hurried back into the building and up the stairs to the Seekers office. He didn't go right in, but hovered outside. 'His wives are here . . . they just drew up.'

Kenny Graham flicked at the blinds. He could see Susie and Stella below, and watched as a small man in a dark navy raincoat approached them. Laytham joined Kenny, watching the women.

'Mrs Hazard!' Both Susie and Stella turned to the small balding man in the navy raincoat; both answered at the same time. 'Yes?'

The man showed the repossession order for Susie's car. No hire purchase payments had been received since the initial down payment. Mr Hazard had been given fair warning.

Stella took the baby and headed for the office as Susie haggled and argued, adamant that there were mitigating circumstances. She passed a furtive-looking Al Franks, his bulbous nose buried behind his racing news.

She pushed open the office door. Laytham stepped directly behind her as Kenny, in Mike's chair behind the desk, swung round to face her. 'Morning, Mrs Hazard. How's Mike?'

Stella froze, immediately protective towards the baby. 'What do you want?'

Laytham was so close. He murmured, 'The disk. We want the disk, and we want it now.'

Kenny came closer. 'We know you got it. Now don't make us hurt this little brat – because we will. We've not got the time to play games.'

Stella's heart was pounding, she was fighting an attack of dizziness, afraid she would faint. She gasped out that she had no idea what they were talking about. Kenny pinched her face in his big hand. 'Then find it! You find it, you go over every inch of this dump, or—'

Susie walked in; she was furious. 'He's taken my car! Repossessed it. He took the keys out of my hand, can you believe it?'

The sight of Stella's white face and the two strange men stopped her in her tracks. She looked from one man's face to the other, then to Stella.

'What's going on? Stella?'

'We're friends of Mike's. We just came for a little chat with his widow . . . right?'

Stella nodded, still clutching the carrycot. 'It's all right, Susie. You take the baby—'

'These men threatening you?'

Stella was so scared, she couldn't get the words out. The blanket from the carrycot slipped to the floor, Susie bent down to retrieve it, and Kenny rested his foot across it. He wore filthy two-toned mud-stained sneakers. Back at her flat Susie hadn't been able to see the man's face, she had been too concerned about protecting her unborn baby, but the foot that had kicked her, time and time again, was the same foot that now rested across Mike's blanket. Slowly Susie straightened and then gave a tight, hard smile. She snatched open her bag, trying to get to her portable phone. 'Run for it, Stella, go on – I'm calling the police!'

Stella shouted: 'No, *no don't! Don't call, Susie!*'

Kenny laughed, and knocked the phone out of Susie's hand. 'You heard her. Now, let's not play any more silly games. We're giving you twenty-four hours. We want the disk, then we won't cause any more trouble. But if we don't get it . . .'

As Laytham walked out, Kenny looked down at the baby; it was a beat before he followed, grinning, showing his chipped horrible teeth all the time.

Stella sat down, hugging the baby. Susie kicked the office door shut. The baby was screaming, his tiny face screwed up, his hands clenching and unclenching. Stella soothed him, hugging him tightly, whispering again and again that it was all over, that nobody was going to harm him, and slowly the baby relaxed, sucking at Stella's finger. The sounds of the men's voices had frightened him, even though he was unaware of who they were or what they were shouting. 'Ssh, now, there's a good boy, it's all over now, yes, good boy . . .'

'Are you crazy? That grinning ape – he was the one that kicked me, and *you scream not to call the police!*'

Stella panted, unable to get her breath. The telephone started to ring, ring. Poor Mike began to scream again. Susie glared round the office. Stella quickly put the baby safely in his carrycot on the desk before she, too, began to look around for the phone. It must have been removed from the desk, and now neither of them could see it. The answer message began: 'You have called Seekers Investigation Agency. There is no one available right now. Please leave your name, number and the time you called, and your call will be returned.' As the message played, Stella became more and more frantic, terrified that it might be Mike himself who was calling.

The voice. Hearing Mike's voice shocked Susie deeply. She gave up searching for the phone and rested against the side of the desk. She saw the phone before Stella, on the floor by the window. Half-heartedly she crossed towards it, as Stella spotted it and made a dive.

'No, I'll answer it.'

'Good morning. This is Alan Church from National Westminster Bank, I'm calling to speak to . . .'

Stella waved the phone in her hand, not knowing how to turn off the answer machine. 'Susie, turn it off, please. I have to talk to him, it's the bank manager.'

Susie pressed the record button off. Stella hesitated and then spoke into the phone. 'This is Mrs Hazard. Hello?' She turned back to Susie. 'Er, this is a private call.'

Susie scowled and folded her arms. 'I can wait.'

Stella turned her back to Susie and lowered her voice. 'I'm sorry, what was that?'

Susie tapped her foot. Stella was nodding, nodding, and then she flapped her free hand. 'Pardon? Could you . . . er, repeat that? *What? What? How much?*' She couldn't get her breath, no amount of panting was any help. She half turned to Susie. 'Quick, get the chair. I'm . . . going to . . .'

Stella passed out: one moment on her feet, the next prostrate on the floor. Susie stepped over her and picked up the phone as the caller asked if anyone was there. Susie replied that she was very sorry but Mrs Hazard would have to call him back. She was indisposed.

*

As Stella sipped the water, the colour came slowly back into her cheeks. She still had not said a word. Susie stood in front of her, arms folded again.

'Will you tell me what the hell is going on?'

Stella's voice sounded distant, as if someone else was talking.

'He owes . . . Mike owes . . . fifty thousand pounds at the bank. They are holding his life insurance policy as security.'

Susie gave a snort. 'Oh, I see, it's the insurance pay-out. So, how much have you . . . ?'

Stella shoved the glass back onto the desk. 'Mind your own damned business.'

'Oh, yes? I come in here, two men are obviously scaring the living daylights out of you and *you tell me to mind my own bloody business*! Well, let me get you straightened out. This is *my* business – one of those men beat me up! Now, you had better come clean with me. What is going on?'

Stella tugged at her coat. 'I need some air, I can't stand it in here a second longer.'

They walked across the boatyard, and out along the towpath by the canal until they came to a low wall and sat down. They held the baby between them in his carrycot. Susie stared into the water.

'Twenty thousand quid in the boot of his car! And you put it in your wardrobe, knowing your house has been broken into, the office broken into, my place . . . You not heard of safety deposit boxes?'

Stella hated the way Susie spoke down to her, as if she were a moron. 'I had a lot on my mind.'

Susie kicked at a pebble. 'So those two goons came for the money, is that it? Yes?'

'Whatever way you look at it, with fifty thousand in the red at the bank, that money was mine.'

'Oh, great.' Susie kicked at another pebble. 'So it's yours, it's Mike's . . . Doesn't really matter, does it? You've not got it any more.' She frowned. 'If they took it, what were they after today? Doesn't make sense. Did they take that money?'

'I don't know!'

'What did they say?'

Stella pulled at her coat. 'Well, it's something to do with Mike.'

'I sort of gathered that, Stella. So come on, what did they say to you? Is it about these?'

Stella stared as Susie pulled out of her pocket a stack of betting slips. 'These were in one of the drawers in his desk. Betting slips. Did they come about debts? Does Mike owe them money?'

Stella peered at the slips. 'Are these Mike's? Only as far as I know he never did the horses. My dad did. Mike always used to say it was a mug's game. Where did you find them?'

Susie pursed her lips, took a slow deep breath. 'I just told you, they were in a drawer in his desk, there's a whole bunch of them. Now you tell me he never made bets, but look, there's at least fifteen of them, Coomes betting shops.'

Stella flipped through the yellow slips. 'I don't know, but they're not big bets, are they?'

'No, so chuck them and tell me what those two goons wanted.'

Stella ran her hands through her hair, making it stand up on end. 'Well, they said I – or Mike – had had something belonging to them, and . . . well, he said it was a disk.'

'A disc,' Susie repeated flatly.

'Yes, a disk.'

'A disc? By anyone famous? – Come on, Stella, what are you talking about?'

Stella picked up a half brick and hurled it into the water. 'That is what he said. They wanted a disk, that it belonged to them, and . . . then they threatened me, said if I didn't hand it over, they'd come back.'

Susie sighed. 'So it's in the office?'

'I don't know – God, I don't know what time of day it is, I can't think straight.'

Susie picked up the carrycot. 'Well, that's an understatement. Right, come on, let's go.'

'Where?'

Susie strode off. 'Back to the office, look for that disk.'

Stella trotted after Susie, then stopped in her tracks. She remembered the scrawled writing on the bathroom cabinet. What had it said? She couldn't remember. Disk! Bottom file!

They searched methodically at first then began tossing files out one by one. Stella focused her search on all the bottom drawers of the filing cabinets. Susie found Mike's diary, and began to thumb through it. She sat on the floor as Stella crawled around on hands and knees. 'There's been no entry for the past . . . Susie counted the days, then the weeks. She began to check further back in the diary, finding odd jotted memos and initials. Two names cropped up three or four times: Laytham and Kenny. There was a further reference to a Kenny Graham. Susie fetched a notepad and began to jot down all the recurring names. Then she picked up an old yellow sticker pad and was about to start marking the pages when she saw the imprint left on the last sticker.

'Well, it's not in any of these files,' Stella announced, looking around for another cabinet. 'Are you going to help me or not?'

Susie pressed the ink pad over the yellow sticker label, removed it. She could make out the letters: 'R-O-S-E-M-O-U-N-T' then a blurred 'H' and 'O'. She started searching through the diary again. Suddenly she couldn't see the pages, everything blurred, and she closed her eyes and sighed. 'I'm so tired'

Stella looked up. 'Well, thank God for small mercies. I was beginning to think you were Superwoman. You know, you should rest, have little afternoon naps. I mean, you've just had a baby – that's like undergoing major surgery. Put your feet up and have a little rest.'

Susie shook her head and yawned. 'I'm fine. I just said I felt tired, I didn't say I was near to collapse. Now stop fussing.'

'I'm not fussing. I just said you should take care more. You don't take care of yourself, and a *healthy* mother is a *healthy* baby.'

Susie looked at Stella. 'They teach you that as well, did

they? I don't know where you get some of these sayings from – but, that said, I will have a quick zizz. Pass that cushion, will you?'

Stella threw it to her and Susie lay on the floor, not a 'thank-you', nothing. She just flopped down and shut her eyes. She was deeply asleep within a moment.

Stella continued to search, then made a cup of tea. She carried it back into the office and Susie sat bolt upright. 'Great, just what I fancied. Thanks.'

Stella handed over the cup. 'You were only out about ten minutes. Are you sure you feel all right?'

Susie nodded, and sipped the hot tea. 'Yeah, Churchill used to take quick ten minute zizzes. So did Margaret Thatcher – it's supposed to be very refreshing, more so than if you had a few hours.'

Stella nodded, going back to the kitchen for another cup of tea. She was lucky if she could sleep at all, never mind the odd ten minutes. She was a nervous wreck, but they had made progress. Susie had thanked her for the tea.

Two hours later Susie was sitting cross-legged, surrounded by files and notes. Stella was filthy, she had searched the tops of every shelf, under every shelf, every filing cabinet – but all without success.

'This is interesting,' Susie muttered. 'Mike was not what I'd call busy. 'I've been trying to find the most recent case he was working on. All I've come up with is a list of what I think could be contact meetings, but there's nothing about what he was actually doing. I remember he said he was working on something big, but there's nothing. And no payments in any of the account books apart from . . . three months back. A Mrs James Donald wrote a letter asking Mike to trace her missing daughter. Well, that couldn't be the big case, a missing girl. Two names keep cropping up, though, a Laytham and a Kenny Graham. Oh, and on this sticker I've got an outline of what I think is a location, "Rosemount Ho" – could be hotel. No address, now—'

Stella interrupted her. 'Why don't you give me a hand and look for this disk? They said they were coming back.'

Susie didn't even look up. 'If they come back I'll call the police. Now, Laytham and Graham feature a lot – or their initials do – and in the early part of this year, there was a meeting with a James Donald. Unless that was the Mrs James Donald and her missing daughter.'

Crash! In a fit of frustration and temper Stella pushed over the empty filing cabinet. The noise woke the baby, and Susie got up in a rage. 'That was stupid – you've woken him up!'

Stella was about to sound off again at Susie when she saw it: a small square computer disk taped underneath the bottom drawer of the filing cabinet, not inside it as she had supposed.

'I've got it! *I've found it!*'

Susie looked at the disk, but it meant nothing. It had a TCC logo, Thompsons Computer Company, and some scrawled writing and dates on the label, but that was all.

The telephone rang, and Stella was on it fast just in case it was Mike. This time it was Mr Sidgwick from the insurance company. He asked to see Stella personally, explaining that he didn't really want to discuss the matter on the telephone.

Stella replaced the receiver. 'I've got to go out.'

Susie nodded, and slipped the disk into her own bag. 'Me too. Can you look after Mike?'

'No, I've got an appointment. Where are you going?'

Susie shrugged into her coat. 'I'm going over to my old unit, maybe get some ID on those two men, and ask a friend of mine to check this disk.'

'The police? You're going to the police?'

'Yes, this disk must have something important on it. You've got a car, I haven't any more. Where are you going?'

Stella hesitated. She fully expected Sidgwick to pay out the remainder of Mike's insurance money. Her mind raced; she'd get it in cash, get her ticket to the Costa Brava, pack, see the estate agents. She was mentally calculating how much time she would need to get away – if Susie started to bring in the police she had better make it as fast as possible. Having the baby in tow would slow her down.

'I'm going to see my—' Stella looked up. Susie had already left. She went over to the window, banged on it. Susie turned in the yard and waved.

'Oh, bugger it!' She'd have to take the baby with her. Stella went over to his carrycot. He was fast asleep, he was such a good baby. She touched his cheek lightly. 'I don't mind having you, my little darlin', but your mother's a shocker. We're going to have to have words with her about you. Yes, we are, because it's not right, is it? She's not like me – you'd have to fight me to get me to leave you if you were mine!' Stella leaned over the carrycot and the baby made a light gurgling sound, turning his head in his sleep. She felt such a warmth for him, which didn't quite take her by surprise – but it was almost like a warning.

Stella arrived at Sidgwick's office. He was taken aback by her appearance: not just how dishevelled she looked, but the fact she also seemed to have acquired a baby.

Stella saw him eyeing the carrycot. 'He's not mine, I'm just minding him for – well, for a friend.'

Mr Sidgwick's kindly face showed great concern. He asked if she was well, and Stella nodded. Again, he was taken aback when she gave him a wonderful smile. 'But let's hope I'm going to be a lot better!'

The computer screen showed up Kenneth Earl Graham's record. A petty criminal, he had served three sentences for arson before he was twenty. Juvenile courts, reform school and Borstal. More recently a five-year sentence for grievous bodily harm. Susie jotted down the details as the officer brought up Laytham's record onto the screen. Anthony – Tony – Laytham. Ex-drug-pusher, ex-pimp, ex-fraudster. Last known address, Rosemount Hotel, Soho. Arrested for small-time fraud 1992. Case dismissed for lack of evidence. Arresting officer was Detective Chief Inspector Michael Hazard.

Harry Green walked into the office, a tall handsome DI, and an old friend of Susie's. She turned and smiled. He held up the TCC disk. 'This little baby is way out of our league. It's what they call in the trade a high-grade virus – and before you start asking me any questions, you can take these home, read up on the virus programs. This one is very sophisticated, we can't use it.'

Susie was handed a stack of magazines, brochures, and back issues on computer viruses and computer frauds.

'We've got no one who can decipher it, you'd have to get a virus specialist. Scotland Yard have set up a unit dealing with computer virus disks. I can give you a contact there, just tell him I put you onto him.'

Susie smiled gratefully. 'Thanks.' She turned back as the officer working on Graham and Laytham gestured for her to come back to the screen.

'Kenny Graham's last known address was the same as Laytham's: Rosemount Hotel. If Laytham's got anything to do with it, it'll be a knocking shop. What was the other name again?'

Susie flicked through her notebook. 'James Donald, possibly living in the Kingston/Richmond area . . . Any luck? Try Surbiton.'

Harry leaned on the back of the uniformed officer's chair. 'I was sorry to hear about old Mike. What made him do it?'

Susie bristled. 'He drowned. Suicide was not proven.'

'Yeah, I know. Strange there wasn't a high level of alcohol recorded. I mean, was he pissed?'

Susie gave a sarcastic half-laugh. 'Oh, you been checking up, have you?'

Harry backed off. 'No, no. Just – word gets out and, well, Mike didn't seem the kind of bloke that'd jump off some bridge into a canal. Was he working on that disk thing?'

Susie bowed her head. 'No. It's just a case I might be looking into. I'm taking over his agency.' Harry put a hand on her shoulder. 'I couldn't believe it at first, no note, nothing. He had debts, but when didn't he? There was no sign of violence, no ID on him, just one of his, I mean, one of the agency cards.'

Harry nodded and rubbed Susie's neck in a familiar way. 'Who ID'd the body?' he asked nonchalantly, eyes focused on the screen.

'Stella, his wife.' Susie stared at the screen, uncomfortable – especially with Harry so close, rubbing her neck. It made her hair stand on end.

'Did he have a big life insurance policy?'

Again Harry didn't appear on the surface to be pushing for information, but Susie recognized this tactic, knew it well, the over-casual question and answer technique. She shrugged. 'I don't think so . . . but obviously he had one, had to have one for collateral to open the agency.'

Susie inched away from Harry and bent closer to the screen. 'Anything on this James Donald yet?'

Harry stuffed his hands into his pockets and strolled around the office. 'Mind you, Mike was no dummy. If he had left a suicide note, then he'd know it could jeopardize his insurance pay-out. Did you have a look over the forensic and post-mortem reports?'

Susie shook her head.

'So who's the main beneficiary?' Harry asked.

Susie coughed. 'His wife . . . Stella.'

Harry looked at her, the way she was standing ram-rod straight, her hands gripping the computer files. She seemed very vulnerable, yet completely unapproachable. 'Ah, well, maybe Mike did just take the easy way out – he could have been nicked for bigamy, never mind anything else.'

Susie glared at Harry, her face tightened. 'Lay off me, just shut it!'

Harry lifted his hands in mock apology. 'Eh, I'm only trying to help. Don't bite my head off.'

He stood closer to the screen. 'So what was he working on? I was told he was doing some debt collecting, a bit of heavy armed stuff. That right? Look Susie, you just ease up a bit. Come on, if there is anything you need help with, then I'm around – and the Gov'nor would have you back any day. There'll be some openings here. I'm being moved up West, so are Ron and Brian, fraud squad. I can always put in a word . . .'

Susie shook her head. She didn't fancy going back into uniform, having to climb all the way back up again. It had been hard enough before she left. 'Nope, I'm just going to run the agency like I said. Maybe I will need that offer of help now and again, though, so – thanks.'

Harry began to look over Graham's and Laytham's reports emerging from the printer. 'These are real low-life scum. What was Mike doing involved with them?'

'I don't know, Harry. I am just trying to find a few things out, it's more personal—' Susie was interrupted.

'Got your J. Donald, Susie. James Anthony Donald. He got six months for theft, Thompsons Computer Company. Bloke's well educated, look at his CV – lotta letters after his name.'

Susie leaned in closer.

'First offence, served in open prison.'

Susie turned as the officer pressed for a print-out of the on-screen information. Harry watched it coming through. 'Seems this guy Donald was in the same nick as Graham, but . . .'

Susie joined Harry, irritated that he was taking so much interest.

'Laytham wasn't. Just Graham and Donald. This any help to you?'

Susie scanned the print-outs, but gave nothing away. Harry rested his arm around her shoulder. 'Nobody liked what happened to you, but it was your choice. You made a big mistake.'

Susie eased away, reaching for her handbag as an excuse. 'That's your opinion, Harry. I happened to be in love with him. Now I've got his kid.'

'He was rotten, Susie, I tried to warn you off him.'

Susie wanted to get out. She hated the way they were all looking at her, asking her such personal questions. 'Thanks for all your help, I really appreciate it.'

But Harry wouldn't let it drop. He walked ahead of Susie to the door. 'Mike was rotten, everybody who came into contact with him got burned. You just won't admit it – he was bent! Somebody had to point the finger at him, he'd been duckin' and divin' for years and everybody knew it. Don't think he took the fall for anyone else, Mike was doctoring evidence as far back as when I first joined here, and he was still doctoring evidence – that stuff you've just taken, Hazard was the arresting officer, and—'

Susie opened the door; she couldn't bear to hear any more. She turned to face the men in the room. 'Like I said, thanks for your help. And, Harry, thanks for looking out all this material for me. You know everybody makes mistakes – and maybe I did – but at the same time it was my choice, and I chose Mike. Now I have his son, he's called Mike . . . after his dad! *Goodnight!*'

The officer shut down his computer. His two friends, who had been working on their own business but listening to the entire interaction, now looked on as he asked Harry if he felt there was something dodgy about the drowning. Mike Hazard was, as everybody knew, a bad apple. But he had been a very well-liked man, a great boozer, great man for showing the new recruits the ropes. 'Mike was a tough bastard,' he said sadly.

Harry became very edgy. 'Yeah, he was a tough bastard – now he's a dead one. If you want some advice, don't get involved. I won't, you know why? I don't want any of his dirt rubbing off on me, and if you start sniffing around it'll create a nasty smell. That clear? Best thing he did was get buried. If she comes back, give me a bell, otherwise stay clear and out of it.'

The young officer lit a cigarette. 'What about his wife?'

Harry was on his way out. 'There's two of them. They can take care of each other.' He shut the door behind him.

There was a tight pause, then the officer returned to the files he had been working on before Susie had arrived. 'I think he fancies her . . .'

The journey from Stoke Newington to Richmond took for ever. Susie was cold, hungry and soaked to the skin, the rain pouring down. She had a tough time opening Stella's garden gate: the latch caught, and she had to shove it hard with her hip. She was so skinny, all the extra pounds she gained before having the baby seemed to have vanished already. Her tall, rangy body was virtually back to normal. She was, and would admit it, even to Stella, feeling more than just tired now, she could hardly keep her eyes open. She might look almost back to normal but she still felt a lot of discomfort and, on the train, she had felt something else. It had taken her by surprise. She suddenly missed the baby – it wasn't a simple emotional feeling of loss, but a deep panic had taken hold of her. Was he safe? Was Stella looking after him? And the panic wouldn't subside. It had lasted for ages, until she had talked herself calm, telling herself that Stella was the safest person in all the world to have left him with, but just to have felt the panic made Susie aware that the bond between her and her baby was growing stronger, deeper.

There was a light on in the downstairs drawing room. Susie could see it through the chink in the curtains, but the hall was in darkness. She pressed the doorbell and leaned against the glass panels to peer in. She heard music, somebody singing; she didn't recognize the tune – maybe it was one of those old warblers, Sinatra or Sammy Davis Junior . . .

Susie rang the bell again, then stepped back out into the rain to look up at the bedroom windows. The upper part of the house was in darkness. She rang once more. She was just beginning to get worried when the hall lights came on. Suddenly she felt good – and then odd, because it *was* odd: she wanted to see Stella, and she wanted to hold her baby, and it felt good to have someone to come home to, someone to tell about all the new developments.

Susie moved closer to the door. 'It's me, Stella, it's Susie.'

Through the stained glass, Susie could just make out a blurred figure. It seemed to bounce from one side of the hall to the other. 'Stella? Are you all right? *Stella, open the door!*'

There was a great deal of fumbling with the latch and chain. Susie pushed the door, it stuck. She pushed again, and Stella tottered backwards.

'Stella? Where's the baby?'

Stella blinked, and then lurched against the wall. 'He's fast asleep, and has been since I put him down, and he's fed, changed, and you are a terrible mother.'

Susie rushed up the stairs and peeked into Mike's room. He was, as Stella had said, sleeping peacefully, a small night-light on, his blankets undisturbed. Susie gently touched his fuzzy head. 'I missed you. There, how about that? Your mama missed you, yes, she did. I'm gettin' better, Mike, aren't I? Do you feel it?'

When Susie went back downstairs the strains of Matt Munro singing 'Softly As I Leave You' on a scratchy old 45 record were playing in the background, Stella had a half pint of Guinness in her hand and her cheeks were flushed. A trail of crisps led from the sitting-room door around the hallway to the front door.

Susie relocked the front door, slipped the latch on. 'Softly As I Leave You' warbled to its conclusion, then began again. She slipped off her wet coat and kicked off her shoes. With just a small lamp on, the room glowed reddish-orange. The coffee table was littered with empty Guinness cans and a fresh six-pack. Stella was by now flat out in an armchair, her feet up on a stool. She was very drunk, her cardigan covered in flakes of broken crisp. She lifted her glass of Guinness to Susie, and wafted the crisp packet. 'I could never drink without a crisp . . . Itsh tha shalt. Salt.'

Susie wanted to go and wrap her arms around Stella, but she didn't. She said quietly, 'Ah! Stella, this won't help.'

She was not in any way prepared for the darker tone, the harsh grating tone to Stella's voice. Cigarette packets and dirty ashtrays were piled high with dog ends. Stella's big wide eyes were dark and angry as she flung the crisps aside. She almost leered at Susie as she rasped out, 'You want a bet? Now get the hell out of *my lounge*!'

CHAPTER EIGHT

Susie had bathed, scrambled some eggs and even washed the dishes – all accompanied by the repeated crackling of 'Softly As I Leave You'. She heard the song end for about the tenth time and waited. There was a longer pause, and she sighed with relief. She was not going to disturb Stella, she felt intuitively this was an off-limits night. Susie had one foot on the stairs when 'Softly As I Leave You' began yet again. She couldn't stand it, whether it was Stella's house or not.

Even more drunk, Stella was still swigging from the Guinness can, a cigarette dangling from her mouth.

'Please, Stella, not again. Why don't you go to bed?'

Stella plonked herself back into the easy chair. 'My house, my record and itshhh my memory . . .' She waved her hand absently – and the can hit the record player. It whizzed round a couple of times along with Matt, then there was an awful scratching sound. Stella staggered up, took the record off the turntable and held it for a moment. 'I'm sorry, Matt, so sorry.' The next moment she smashed the record into pieces and returned to her seat. She opened another can and held it high up in the air. 'Cheers! Mike bought me that record. Miké. It conjures up my teenage years. Ha! Haw haw! I don't think I've played it since I was thirteen or . . .'

Susie sat on the edge of the sofa. She twisted her long delicate fingers, trying to think of the right thing to say.

'It was the proudest day of my father's life when I married Mike – God, that old fool loved him, thought the sun shone out of him! He was the best prop, or was it forward? Played rugby. Yes, Mike was a great rugby player, and I was his sweetheart fan, standing on the touchline blue with cold, not having the faintest – and he never knew this – but I never knew what they were all doing, running up and down with that ball. It's not ball, is it? What do they call it?'

Stella suddenly leaned back and closed her eyes. 'How can you live with a man all those years, Susie, and not know him? Not really know him at all? How can you sleep with a man all these years, and not know who he really is, what he is? How?'

Susie was almost in tears herself. 'I know how you feel.'

'No, you don't,' came the soft, sad reply.

'Of course I do. I loved him and—'

'It's not the same.'

'Yes, it is!' Susie snapped.

'No, it isn't.' But Stella didn't snap back; her tone was dark, deeply angry. 'It's not the same at all. 'I'm menopausal and you're young, you have a child. It is not the same. I am empty. Menopausal is bad enough but I'm broke too. Flat stony broke.'

Susie sighed. She didn't bother replying that so was she. With Stella in this mood there was no point in talking and she was about to walk out when Stella lurched across the room towards a small desk. She fumbled for her glasses, and placed them crookedly on her nose.

'What is it? Have you found something out?' Susie asked.

Stella began tossing papers around the room. 'Oh, I've found out something all right! The small terraced house with paved garden at rear, mortgaged *three* times over . . . and if, *if* payment is not made, the small house'll be repossessed. Then there's the fifty thousand outstanding in the current, the empty, *empty* deposit account, and then there's the life insurance payments, not one paid in the last six months. Life insurance policy null and void, and these—' She threw a fistful of bills into the air. 'Electricity – red. Gas – red. Telephone – red. And the office you're so proud of? Well, the lease is defunct due to non-payment, and – here, have a look at the outstanding bills on that. I'm not in debt. No! No! I'm not in debt! I'm *bankrupt*! Now how do you think I feel? *Tell me! Go on, Miss Smart-arse! You tell me how I am supposed to feel!*'

Susie could not believe it. She picked up the bills, dazed. Stella lit a cigarette, stubbed out the previous one left in the ashtray with all the other dog ends.

114

'My God! I'll never forget this night. You know, I would never have believed him capable of doing anything like this. I must have been blind and, well, as . . .'

Susie had to sit down – she was stunned.

Stella was leaning against the mantelpiece, her back to Susie. She looked up and could see her sitting, head bowed, on the sofa. 'There's something else. I've tried to tell you, God only knows how many times, Susie. About Mike, the funeral.'

'Shut up.'

'No, no, I can't. Please let me get this out.'

'No – you listen to *me*. That disk, the one from the office, I know what it is. It's a virus disk.'

Stella could hardly see Susie – her vision was so blurred – and she was unable to make out what on earth she was talking about. 'Virus?'

Susie went on, 'I know who those two men are, the ones that came to the office, and it's all somehow connected to a James Donald. Something to do with computer fraud. I think that's the big case Mike was working on, some kind of computer fraud . . .'

Stella clutched at the mantelpiece. 'I think . . . do you mind helping me up to the bathroom? I'm going to be sick.'

Susie helped Stella to bed. She had been very sick, and all she could think about was lying down. The room, everything, was spinning round and round.

But it was worse in the morning. She was unable even to lift her head. Pain thudded across her eyes, her whole body seemed to ache. Susie, on the other hand, was even more determined now to get to the bottom of the mystery surrounding the disk, as if it were some kind of clue to all the terrible things Mike had done. She was desperate to piece together the jigsaw, certain that when she had done so she would find all the answers.

She was becoming more adept with the baby, and had bathed, changed and fed him without assistance from Stella. She even ran Stella's bath and fetched her black coffee and aspirin.

The slam of the car door made Stella wince. The baby, clad in his little blue teddy-bear suit, was held in a sling round her neck.

'Where are we going, if it's not a rude question? It's just that under the circumstances I think maybe I should remain at home. I've got to sell that house, get some money to pay off—'

'We are going to visit Mrs Donald, the woman who asked Mike to trace her missing daughter. We are going to talk to this James Donald and find out what's been going on.'

They drove in silence. Every time Susie braked, Stella's head gave an agonizing thud. It's only half past eight. Isn't this a bit early to go visiting someone we don't know?'

Susie answered, 'We are not paying a social call. This is business. You can stay in the car if you want, I just thought that maybe you would be as interested as I am in trying to find out what made Mike do what he's done to you and to me.'

Stella nodded, wincing. 'Well, we should get that disk back to those two men. They frightened the life out of me!'

Susie drew up outside a neat semi-detached house in Surbiton.

'Don't bang the door!' Stella pleaded. 'It's my head.'

'Why don't you just stay in the car?' said Susie acidly.

But Stella followed her up the path, Mike tucked in the babysling. Susie rang the front door bell. Stella jiggled Mike up and down. 'We don't look very professional.'

Susie flicked at one of the blue ears on Mike's teddysuit. 'I hate that thing. How many of them have you got?'

Mrs Donald was nervous, uncertain at first whether or not to let them in. Stella witnessed the policewoman side of Susie at first hand and was impressed. She was very cordial, showing the Seekers card, explaining that she worked alongside Mike Hazard, that she was his wife. That last part irritated Stella, as did also that *she* seemed to be treated like the home help.

The immaculate lounge was fussy and over-filled with

116

knick-knacks. Mrs Donald offered tea or coffee. Stella was just about to say she'd love one, when Susie declined. 'I think I'd prefer to get down to finding out some more facts. Now, you contacted Mike Hazard to trace your daughter?'

Mrs Donald explained that Sherry, her fifteen-year-old, had run away from home on numerous occasions before. Previously, she had always returned; the last time a social worker had intervened, and she had been certain that Sherry would not run away again. But she had, and now Mrs Donald was scared that if she informed the social worker they might make Sherry go into some kind of home. Mrs Donald constantly twisted a paper tissue round and round. She cried easily, plucking at her neat pleated skirt. 'My husband didn't get on with Sherry. They did nothing but argue.'

Susie had a concerned look on her face, nodding, encouraging Mrs Donald to talk. 'So did you contact Mr Hazard yourself? Or did your husband?'

'Oh, he came here, he was working with Jim and it was Jim who suggested that I talk to Mr Hazard. Then he said that Mr Hazard would need a formal request, photographs. Do you have the photograph?'

Mrs Donald passed over the photograph of a pretty, dark-haired girl. 'Mr Hazard assured me he would find her, but I've heard nothing.'

Susie was standing, looking around the room. 'But Mr Hazard met with your husband before your daughter went missing?'

'Yes. They used to go out back to the workshop.'

Susie looked at Stella, gave her a tiny wink. 'Could I speak to your husband, please? It's very urgent.'

Mrs Donald shook her head. 'I don't know where he is. You see there was a terrible fire at the factory where he used to work. The police called round, looking for him, but I told them I hadn't seen him for weeks, and—'

'And?' Susie interrupted.

'I said to them, "I don't want to see him." We had this terrible row about Sherry – awful. He's not her real father, he's her stepfather. They used to get on so well when she was

117

small, but . . . I just want Sherry home, Mrs Hazard, can you help me find her?'

Susie was led into the back garden, telling Stella to stay with the baby in the lounge. Again Stella felt annoyed. She'd not said one word. It was difficult for her: Susie in her police-woman guise, interviewing Mrs Donald, was like a stranger. Stella was left to feel just like a babyminder. She was going to tackle Susie about it.

Mike started to cry and Stella rose to walk him up and down the room. He'd be due for a feed any minute. She traipsed backwards and forwards on the floral carpet, crossing to the fireplace, gasping for a coffee. Mike was getting desper-ate now, so she tried holding up an ornament to distract him, waving it in the air. He was totally uninterested and screaming with hunger.

It was then Stella noticed the photograph of James Donald. He was standing next to his wife in the silver frame, and Stella knew instantly that it was the man she had buried. She started to pant, pant – and had to sit down on the sofa. Her head was throbbing . . .

Susie checked over the shed used as Donald's workshop. She noticed the stack of computer disks had the same logo as the one found at the office: TCC. She looked at the box.

'So your husband worked at Thompsons Computer Com-pany? He was charged with some kind of fraud, wasn't he?'

Mrs Donald turned away. 'I don't know anything about his work, but he was very upset when they sold out. You see, he was supposed to be a partner, they just used his ideas, and programs. I think it's not called Thompsons any more, those disks would be from the time he worked there, before . . .'

Susie's eyes roamed the hut. 'I know about your husband's prison sentence. What was he doing, do you think? Making some kind of virus disks?'

'I don't know anything about his work, just – just that after prison he was a changed man, and—'

'And?' Susie asked sharply.

'Well, there were these men . . . I never knew who was in and out of here. They'd come in via the garden, and – I can't really see what on earth this has to do with you finding Sherry.'

'I need to speak to your husband. Have you any idea where he could be? Perhaps Sherry is with him?'

'*No!* No, I don't think you understand. Sherry wouldn't be with her father, she hated him!'

Susie walked out to the car through the garden as Mrs Donald showed Stella out of the front door. Stella felt wretched, she wanted to say something – anything – to make the poor woman happier. 'We'll find your daughter. I'm so sorry, I am really very sorry . . .'

Mike was really howling and nothing seemed to quieten him. His crying made Stella's headache even worse. She was in need of an aspirin, Andrew's Liver Salts. She felt terrible. Susie pressed the car horn, Stella jumped, and her head started to throb violently. 'There was no need to do that! What if he was asleep?'

Susie peered at the baby. 'Well, he obviously isn't, so let's get him a bottle, or does he need changing?'

As Stella eased the carrycot into the back seat and then sat in the passenger seat, another thing niggled her about Susie. This was Stella's car, and yet Susie just got in without even asking if she could drive, and Stella seemed to be the one always left with Mike, especially if he was crying, as he was now.

'I would appreciate you not treating me like the au pair! If there's one thing I can't stand, it's people who toot their car horn. I was coming as fast as I could, the poor woman was in floods of tears and Mike wouldn't stop crying.' Stella looked around. 'Are we going home? He's not happy at all.'

She looked at Mike, but he seemed to have cried himself to sleep. She tucked in his blanket. Susie looked at him through the driving mirror. 'I was going to take you both home, but as he's nodded off, we'll go to the factory where Donald worked. I know there's a link, I just feel it in my water.'

'I could have done with a glass of water, a cup of coffee, anything – but you just said no! I'm gasping.'

Susie left Stella in the car as she went in to speak with the security guard on duty. The makeshift hut was positioned by the gates of Thompsons Computer Company. The entire building had been reduced to a blackened, burnt-out shell.

Stella had to get out of the car to walk Mike up and down, then she fed him and settled him on the back seat in his carrycot. Susie was in the security hut for almost fifteen minutes. She shot out like a bullet.

'Right! Listen to this, there was a fire here, arson suspected. Kenny Graham has served time for arson, that's one point. The police have been over the place like ants. The whole place went up . . . two men working in the rear left side of the building, where all the highly flammable chemicals were stored, died. A third man was trapped on the second floor. He was taken to Richmond burns unit. Guess what night the fire broke out?'

'I don't know but I'm sure you're going to tell me! I thought you'd come out of his hut and announce your engagement to the bloke. You've been in there long enough.'

'He was having his coffee break.'

'Oh, very nice. Did you have one?'

Susie turned in exasperation. 'I don't believe you! Look how it's all coming together. The man working with Mike on that computer virus disk was James Donald, right? He used to work at this factory, he was sentenced to six months for fraud. Now, Kenny Graham was in the same nick as Donald, so that's how they link together. What if Donald, when he was in the nick, talks to Kenny about virus disks, who gets out and talks to Laytham? Now I'm not sure how Mike fits into all this, but he was also with Donald *before* his daughter went missing, so that wasn't the reason he was at Donald's house and in that workshop.'

'I can't follow this at all. What's a virus disk?'

120

'I've told you, I showed you the magazines. It's a disk that if you put it into a computer it does something to the programs.'

'Like what?'

'*I don't know!*'

Stella shook her head. 'Well, at last there's something the brain of Britain isn't sure of!'

Susie looked hard at Stella. She could have slapped her. 'One thing I am certain of: that man in the fire at this factory is James Donald. So that's our next stop.'

Stella stepped back, suddenly scared. She knew the man in the fire couldn't be James Donald. She remembered the inspector saying how he'd found Mike's car near to a factory fire . . . and she hadn't identified James Donald until the next day. It wasn't James Donald in the fire, or at Richmond. Stella had more reason to think it was Mike himself.

'I am not going to the hospital,' Stella said stubbornly.

Susie was half in and half out of the car. 'What?'

'I am not going. I have personal effects to sort out, my bank situation, the reservation for the Costa Brava, the estate agents. My business is more important.'

Susie looked at Stella as if she was a moron.

'And don't you look at me like that! You're the most irritating woman I have ever met. Most women when they have a baby have post-natal depression – but *you* – you've got a dose of aggression. You cart that baby here, there and everywhere. You're a terrible mother! Newborn babies shouldn't be dragged around the place in the back of cars, you've got all the fumes, the noise, the—'

'Prattle on, Stella, I'm getting used to turning a deaf ear. How Mike put up with it for all those years God only knows. No wonder he left you for someone he could at least have a sane conversation with—'

The backhander would have been applauded by the group of workmen who had downed tools to watch the two women at the roadside – but better was to come. Susie snarled, hand to her jaw, 'Don't you ever hit me again! You try it and I'll knock you through that wall.'

The punch came next, a good straight wallop to the chin.

121

Susie teetered backwards, regained her balance and leaned forward to feel her jaw again. She looked at Stella in stunned amazement, then moved just that bit closer so that the upper cut would make contact. The men burst into applause as Stella was lifted off her feet, and landed flat on her back in the road. She raised her head, blood streaming from her nose.

Susie felt terrible. At first she turned away, ashamed to have lost her cool to such an extent. She turned back just as Stella sat up, touching her bloody nose and then looking up at Susie almost with awe.

Susie proffered her hand. 'Come on, this is crazy. Gimme your hand.' She hauled Stella to her feet.

'My God, you punched me. At full strength, too. I held back, I didn't give you all I'd got,' Stella said, and spun round to the still gawping group of workmen. 'You had your eyeful? Get back to work, you lazy so-and-sos!'

Stella remained in stony silence throughout the drive to Richmond hospital. She had almost resigned herself to Susie discovering the truth: Mike had been dead and now he was burnt up in a hospital ward. 'God moves in a mysterious way,' she muttered.

'Pardon?' Susie said, as she slammed the car door for the tenth time that day.

'Will you *please* not slam the door, you'll wake the baby up. You shouldn't even be parked here. This is a doctor's bay.'

Susie was heading towards the reception area. 'Drive it around, then. Anyone asks you to move, just move.'

'Oh, thanks. I can drive my own car then, can I?' Stella walked round to the driver's side, eased open the door and squashed herself into the seat. She checked the baby, and looked over to the main hospital entrance. She turned on the radio very low and sat back. Any minute now, she told herself, Susie's going to come out of there like a bat out of hell. She half wondered if they'd have another punch-up.

She sat bolt upright as Susie rapped the window, but Stella

122

was sitting tight, this was *her* car and she was fed up with being driven around by Susie. Besides, if she was going to get another punch she was better off in the driving seat – she could just take off. But Susie didn't look angry or upset: quite the reverse. She was excited.

'You're not going to believe this. James Donald – I was right, it was him, and he was here!'

Stella frowned. Had she got the days and times wrong?

'He was here until he discharged himself. They couldn't believe it, the doctor said he had third degree burns to his hands and chest and the right side of his head. He said—'

'He discharged himself? You mean he just walked out?'

Susie nodded. 'Yeah, well, if he'd torched the factory, he'd be scared. The doctor said the police had been trying to interview him. OK, now we go to the Rosemount Hotel.'

'What?'

'It's the hotel in Soho, the one run by Tony Laytham – aren't you following anything I've told you? It was in the yellow pad, the address, I told you that when I went to the police station they told me—'

'Oh, yes, that their last address was the same hotel. Well, I'm sorry, but you can't use my car.'

Susie did a slow, very slow, turn towards Stella. 'What?'

'I have to get to the estate agent's and get a board up. I have things to do and I need my car. I do not have the time or inclination to go to any Rosemount Hotel. Er, what street is it in?'

'Greek Street, Soho. And fine, you don't wanna go, don't!'

'Good.' Stella sighed. Now she was sure it had been Mike in the fire, and now it was possibly Mike who was hiding out with those two terrible men. 'And I think you should go to the office with the disk, and when they come, you give it to them.'

'Oh, that's what you think, is it? Well, you go home, you do whatever you have to do. I would be very grateful if you could take Mike with you as *you* have the car.'

'Where are you going?'

Susie slammed the car door for the eleventh time. 'I'll get the tube. See you later.'

'Shit!' Stella hit the wheel with her hand. She watched as Susie swung her handbag over her shoulder, head up, and almost marched along.

Stella started the engine. 'Well, I've not driven in the West End since nineteen eighty-five, Mike, but we'd better get to this hotel before your mother. Now, what was it again? The Rosemount . . . and it was Greek Street. Now I know that's off Shaftesbury Avenue . . .'

Stella talked to herself all the time she was driving. She remembered her old driving instructor telling her it was the best method to keep panic from making her a danger on the road. She had failed four driving tests and the poor man had retired, early, from some nervous condition.

'I think he got anorexia nervosa, Mike, it was something like that, couldn't eat. Oh, he got so thin, I was always worried about him, you know, that he'd pass out while he was teaching me to drive. He did once, but that was when I hit that woman on the level crossing – well, not her, not exactly, I just clipped her wheelie shopping trolley. But he got into a terrible state. I think we'll go via Chiswick roundabout, I know that route, straight down the Cromwell Road. Yes. Just say a few Hail Marys, Mike, that I get to this Rosemount Hotel before your mother. Mind you, the rate she was striding down the road, she'll probably run the entire distance.'

In room eleven of the Rosemount Hotel Mike Hazard was sleeping in wretched agony. His hands were unbearably painful and, although the burns to his face and ear were healing, the wounds on his chest continued to weep and he knew they were becoming badly infected. The door was locked, day and night. Trapped in the squalor of the hotel room he had had time to realise what a stupid fool he'd been. He hoped that somehow Stella would have got to the disk – it was his passport out. He reckoned it could all still work, but he had somehow to get out of the building and get to the disk. Then it would all be

124

OK – he'd finally scoop the big-time money he dreamed of. He could still be rich.

Susie arrived at Earls Court station to change to the Piccadilly line. There was a delay and she waited for almost half an hour, unable to decide whether she should get out of the station and grab a taxi or just sit tight.

Stella got lost in the one-way system around Piccadilly Circus. She passed the Shaftesbury Avenue turn-off twice in the wrong lane, and her nerves were in shreds by the time she headed down Wardour Street and at last turned into Soho Square, which she knew, and half-way round hit Greek Street. She couldn't believe her luck as mid-way down she spotted an empty meter, even though she hadn't seen this Rosemount Hotel. She held up the traffic as she attempted to park, then suffered near heart failure when she saw the charge was twenty pence for six minutes. My God, had it been that long since she was in the West End? Twenty pence for just six minutes?

Stella had to stop six passers-by before she was able to make up half an hour on the meter. Nobody seemed to have a twenty pence piece. Finally she reached in for Mike, and through the car window she suddenly caught sight of a girl opposite her on the pavement, wearing shorts, striped tights, platform shoes and a leather jacket. The girl was smoking as she chatted to a bloke, then she took off. Stella locked the car as fast as she could, hampered by carrying the baby and her handbag. She hurried off after the girl, somehow sure that she was Sherry Donald, the missing girl Mike Hazard had been hired to find.

Even with the platform shoes Sherry was moving fast. Down Greek Street, past the Groucho Club. Then she was walking along old Compton Street. By this time Stella had the photograph out and she was certain that the young, confident girl ahead of her was Sherry.

Stella caught up with Sherry as she waited to cross over from Wardour Street into Berwick Street. Sherry was laughing with a girl not much older than herself, who had a punk haircut and wore a black leather mini skirt. She looked cold, wearing just a skinny T-shirt, no jacket, and Sherry slipped an arm around her shoulder. Stella was almost within touching distance, but then Sherry was off again, ducking and diving across the road into Berwick Street. Stella kept up her chase, but was finally defeated by all the fruit and vegetable stalls in the market.

The girls were entering a sleazy strip club. Red-striped plastic curtains fluttered at the open doorway, a red light glowed inside the club. The adverts proclaimed 'Live Sex Shows', and pictures of nude girls in typical lewd, sexy poses were displayed in show cases either side of the entrance. It was, however, the sign above the club's entrance that made Stella stop dead in her tracks. A neon sign, half broken, but the flash-flash of its lights could still attract the punters: The Rosemount Hotel.

CHAPTER NINE

The interior of the club-cum-seedy-hotel was so badly lit that Stella could barely distinguish whether or not it was Sherry who stood behind a small reception desk.

'Excuse me . . .'

Stella had another quick look at the photograph as the young girl turned. She'd been replacing keys on a rack behind the desk.

'Are you Sherry Donald?'

Sherry's mouth pursed; she looked over-made-up, wearing too much eye-shadow and mascara. 'Who are you?'

'You are, aren't you? Sherry?'

Sherry looked past Stella to the doorway. 'You a bleedin' social worker?'

'No, no, I'm not. Please, just listen to me.'

Sherry lit a cigarette. Her bitten-down fingernails were painted a brilliant crimson. Stella leaned on the counter, the weight of the baby in her arms giving her backache. 'Sherry, I'm not a social worker, honestly – but I'm a friend of your mother's.'

'I ain't goin' back. You're not gettin' me back wiv him!'

'Will you just call your mother? She's worried sick about you. Please, just one phone call to say you're—'

'Oh, all right. Now you'd better get out of here – I'm workin'.'

Stella jiggled the baby as he started to whimper. 'There's just one other thing, then I'll go. Is someone staying here?'

Sherry unwrapped some chewing gum. 'Nah! It's not a real 'otel. Look, you'd better go, you'll get me in trouble. Go on.' She had a thick Cockney accent; with her cigarette and now her chewing gum she was over-confident, aggressive. 'Get out.

127

I'll call her – all right wiv you if I do it in me own time?'

Stella looked towards the narrow corridor. There was a staircase and she stepped towards the archway.

'You can't go in there! Get out!' Sherry screeched.

'Is there a tall man, dark-haired – big man? Have you seen him? I mean, could he be using one of the rooms?'

Sherry slammed round from her desk. 'No! You got to go!'

Just then the young girl Stella had seen Sherry talking to earlier came down the stairs, followed by a scruffy middle-aged man. She flounced out as he scuttled after her.

'I got customers – tarra, Joleen, see you later.'

Joleen, still in her skinny-rib T-shirt, pulled a face as she swished the plastic curtain aside. 'Laytham's comin' down the street, Sherry, look busy!'

Stella caught hold of Sherry's hand. 'Laytham? Did she say Laytham?'

The baby started to fidget. Sherry was about to push Stella out.

'Please, could I have a glass of water? I'm not feeling well . . .' Sherry sighed, then gestured to a dark maroon-coloured curtain directly behind her desk. 'Go in there. It's the kitchen, but stay in there, me boss is comin'. Go on.'

Stella hurried behind the curtain, just missing Laytham as he walked into his club. She looked round the disgusting kitchen. It was filled with dirty cups and glasses, greasy take-away cartons and stale milk bottles. Through the shabby curtain she could just make out Laytham standing by the desk, checking over the day's takings. She couldn't quite hear what they were saying, as music had started up, and two more girls arrived with their customers and headed up the stairs to the rooms.

Kenny Graham appeared next to Laytham, and by now Stella was having her usual palpitations. She didn't dare set foot outside the curtain in case she was seen. She kept on patting Mike's back, petrified he would start crying – it was coming up to his feed time.

Kenny reached over the desk and took the key to room eleven. He had some take-away food in a bag, and was about to start for the stairs when Laytham turned to him. 'I'll take that up. You go and get the car round.'

Kenny handed over the food and the room key. Laytham pushed his black hat up onto his forehead. 'Business is lookin' like a dog's dinner. How many girls been in today, Sherry?'

Sherry was really nervous, flicking looks to the curtain, terrified the woman with the baby would walk out. Laytham clipped her hard across the face. 'Eh! Listen to me when I'm talkin' to you. I said—'

She stepped away from him. 'Four. We've had just four since we opened.'

Laytham swore as he headed for the stairs. He turned as little Joleen returned with another punter and sighed: the slags were gettin' too cheap-looking, he'd have to have a word with her to smarten up her appearance.

Laytham went up to the second floor landing. He unlocked the door, threw a furtive look back down the stairs, and entered the dark squalid room.

Mike Hazard lay on his side, fully clothed, his face turned to the wall.

'Here's some nosh,' Laytham said as he banged the take-away curry on the dressing table. 'Mike? Eh! You hear me? You awake?'

Laytham moved closer to the bed. 'Did Kenny give you the clean bandages and disinfectant? Mike?'

Hazard lay motionless. Laytham tossed his hat aside, he knelt on the side of the bed to turn him over. 'Mike? For chrissakes, don't you bleedin' die on us! Mike?'

Laytham tried to feel for Hazard's pulse. Mike slowly opened his eyes, looked at Laytham – then jerked forward, hard. His forehead smacked into Laytham, who lost his balance and fell onto the floor. He made a frantic attempt to stop himself from falling, grabbing desperately first at the cover of the bed, and then at Mike's legs, but Mike was up. He kicked Laytham away, then grabbed a heavy glass ashtray.

Sherry was searching for condoms behind her desk when Laytham walked past her, hat pulled down, coat collar turned up.

'We're out of the fruit-flavoured ones, Mr Laytham, we need some more stock and—'

Laytham didn't even turn towards her but swiped the striped curtain aside and disappeared. Stella saw him go, and knowing Kenny wasn't there she hurried out, just as Susie appeared at the door.

'Stella! What are you doing here?'

Stella grabbed Susie. 'Out! Go on, hurry, just get out, I'll explain.'

Susie jerked her arm free, because she had now spotted Sherry. 'Wait – aren't you Sherry Donald?'

'*Yes. Yes*, she is, but come on, out, hurry. It's Laytham's place.'

Susie was furious as Stella dragged her out onto the pavement. Stella looked up and down the road, fearful that Kenny Graham would appear at any moment. 'Just get away from this place, I'll fill you in. I got a meter . . . come on!'

As they headed back towards Berwick Street market, Stella explained that she had felt guilty about not driving Susie, so had tried to catch her up, then driven straight to Soho. It all tumbled out in a garbled torrent – how she had asked Sherry to call her mother, and how Sherry promised that she would . . . Susie halted abruptly. 'What about Donald? Is he in the hotel? If Sherry's there then he must be with her.'

'No, there was no one staying and—'

'How do you know?' Susie interrupted.

'Because I asked, and then Laytham came in.'

They were heading across Wardour Street now, when a police car with siren screaming sped past them. By the time they reached the Golf, another police car with lights flashing was seen hurtling down Old Compton Street.

Stella surrendered the car key to Susie, who drove them off down towards the end of Greek Street. There she glimpsed Sherry Donald, running like a scared rabbit down Wardour Street. Susie followed and slowed the car alongside her. 'Sherry! Are you all right?'

Sherry was in a panic, she flapped her hands, but couldn't speak. Susie stopped the car and got out, pushing her seat forward. 'Come on, in you get.'

Sherry didn't argue, she almost dived into the back seat. 'Go on! Hurry – get out of here – drive! *Drive!*'

Susie started off down Wardour Street again, looking at Sherry in the driving mirror. She was crying, mascara-laden tears streaming down her cheeks.

'What happened?'

'I dunno, but Laytham come back, right, he went upstairs . . . and then there was all this screaming! Joleen saw him, he was covered in blood, somebody had smashed his head in. The filth was there in seconds, I never seen nuffink like it, I just scarpered. *What you stoppin' for?*'

Susie turned to Sherry. 'Just calm down. Was it your father?'

Sherry gaped. 'What you talkin' about? It was Tony Laytham, somebody done him in. Oh, God almighty, I'm gonna be in terrible trouble!'

'Just calm down and explain it to me.'

'I'm under age, they'll put me in a home.'

Stella nudged Susie to start driving again. 'Have they taken him to hospital?'

'He was dead. Somebody walked in and – oh, my God! Me mum will go barmy about this!'

Susie and Stella stood waiting outside a public toilet. Sherry had wanted to wash off her make-up and tidy herself up before facing her mother. Susie was finally giving Mike his bottle.

'Well, that gives us a bit more time. If Laytham's dead, I mean, he won't be waiting at the office for the disk. We got to find out what's on it.'

Stella sighed. 'There may not be any connection. Personally I think we're getting involved in something we should just walk away from. Just – just let them have it, if they still want it. Post it to the hotel – anything. If Sherry's telling the truth, somebody just walked in and murdered Laytham. They're terrible people.'

'Why would she lie? And I think her father is involved. I think he may have been hiding out at that hotel. Maybe it was her father who murdered Laytham. *Where are you going?*'

'She's been too long in there. I'll just check up, she may have tried to run away.'

Susie was impressed. 'Oh, good thinking. OK.'

Sherry was slumped against the wall, crying her heart out. She didn't seem like the same cocky teenager from the hotel. 'I don't wanna go back home, I hate him! I don't wanna face him. It's nothin' to do with Mum, she's just stupid – but me dad. Please, don't make me go home.'

Stella bent forward and touched Sherry's head. 'Sherry, what if I was to promise you that your father's never coming home, that you're going to be safe and looked after? Your mother is very worried, and she loves you.'

Slowly Sherry got to her feet. 'How can you promise me that?'

Stella hesitated. 'Because – well, because I am an investigator, and we know certain things about people. Your father isn't coming back.'

Sherry suddenly gave a wonderful cheeky grin. 'Oh, that's great! OK then, I come home wiv you. I don't know your name even. What's your name?'

'I'm Mrs Hazard. Stella.'

'Oh, and who's the other woman? Is that her baby?'

'Yes. She's Susie.'

Susie was examining the disk as Sherry climbed into the back seat. She looked at Susie, then to the disk. 'Oh, is that how you know me dad? You work wiv him, do you? That's one of his, innit? Eh – hang on a second, you're not cops, are you?'

Susie started the car. 'No, but I run an investigation agency, and we are interested in this disk. We think your father made it.'

Sherry leaned with both elbows between the front seats. 'What was he up to this time? You know he got a prison sentence for fraud? He done a virus disk at his old factory – the accounts department didn't know nuffink, they was paying him an extra five hundred quid a month! He wouldn't have been sussed, but the factory got sold, see, they got new accountants in and he was nicked.'

They drove on. After a moment Susie asked Sherry if she knew anything about virus disks. 'I dunno, I'd have to run it through the computer first. You sure me dad's not coming back?'

Stella coughed, trying to change the subject, but Mike changed it for her: he suddenly started howling and Sherry's attention was drawn to him. 'Oh, innee *lovely*! Can I 'old 'im?'

Susie said that she could and, as they were nearly at Mrs Donald's house, she was allowed to take him out of his carrycot.

Sherry carried Mike up the path. Stella followed with his bottle and the carrycot, while Susie remained behind to lock up the car. 'A minute, Stella.' She used that frosty tone, and Stella stopped.

Susie lowered her voice. 'Working with me, you *never* make promises you cannot keep, do you understand? What was that about Donald never coming home?'

Stella's lips tightened with anger. 'I'm not working, Susie. I'm trying to get my life back together, and I never said a word to her about anything.' She was getting good at telling lies. It surprised her, she hadn't even blushed.

Sherry sat at one of her father's computers. The small workshop out in the back garden was filled with different models and printers. Boxes of equipment were stacked everywhere, and a long table was piled with what appeared to Stella to be the insides of televisions or radios. Old filing cabinets lined a wall from floor to ceiling, adapted to take row upon row of disks. Other walls were lined with bookshelves and magazine racks, everything connected to the computer world.

Stella had time to look over the makeshift office-cum-workshop because she had been there for more than an hour as Sherry sat at the desk. Sometimes Sherry looked just like a schoolkid, an intense look on her young face, but she swore like a navvy, and smoked throughout, flicking the ash with her bitten-down fingernails. At times it was difficult to decipher what she was saying, her accent was so strong. Stella found that strange: Mrs Donald was rather affected, a bit posh, and made sure every H was articulated, whereas Sherry appeared not to realize they existed in the English language.

'Cor blimey, I'm 'avin' a 'ard time wiv this, nuffink makes sense. Lemme try somefink else, give us that batch of disks there, Susie. Ta. Oh, yeah, now I'm gettin' somefink up. Funny, not a lot of it makes any common – know what I mean?'

Susie was on a small stool, sitting lower down than Sherry, who was perched on her dad's swivel seat. She tapped and flicked, her bitten nails flying over the keyboard, eyes straining to the screen. Susie had no idea what she was doing, but was glued to the screen almost as intently as Sherry.

They all jumped as Mrs Donald's voice boomed: 'Tea's on the table, everybody.'

Sherry swivelled across to one side of the desk and flicked on a switch. 'We'll be in in a minute.' She turned back again. 'I fink I'm gettin' there. 'Ang on – shit! It's done it again!' She jerked her thumb back to the speaker on the wall, connected to the house. 'That's how she found out about me dad! I left it on, see, so she heard him fumblin' around with me. He was disgusting, I 'it 'im, but 'e wouldn't stop, sweatin' and pantin' over me. It was disgustin', but – holy shit, will you look at this!'

All they could see on the screen was a row of dots. Susie craned forwards, Stella kissed the top of Mike's head as she, too, looked at the screen. 'Don't you think we should go in for tea?' she suggested.

'I'm not hungry,' Susie said.

Stella paced up and down again. Mike yawned, his little legs and arms stretched and then he sucked his fist. Sherry's description of her father was hideous. Stella remembered how Mrs Donald had repeated over and over how she never wanted to see him again, that there had been a terrible row. Now she knew what it must have been about. James Donald had tried to molest his own stepdaughter. Sherry, for all her bravado, was really just a child.

'Bleedin' 'ell, you gotta 'and it to the bastard, he's a fuckin' genius! This is breakin' codes, see, I got the disk you 'ad in one side, and I'm using another off the main 'ard disk, and it's distortin' it . . . It's wipin' it clean!'

Mrs Donald bleeped in on the loudspeaker to say again that tea was on the table. Sherry reached over and flicked the switch. 'I'm comin'. Shut up!'

Susie was still glued to the screen. She didn't understand about hard disks and soft disks. 'What is it actually doing?'

Stella felt her stomach rumble. She'd had no lunch, not even a coffee that morning. 'Don't you think we should go in for tea?' she asked again, plaintively.

'I'm not hungry!'

'But Mrs Donald has got everything ready and—'

Susie turned and pointed to her mouth. 'Read my lips, Stella. I am *not hungry*!'

Stella crossed to the door. 'Well, *I*'m not, either – but maybe you should think about your son!' She slammed out.

Sherry didn't pay any attention. She was now tapping, then pressed 'enter', waited, and pressed 'enter' again. 'OK, now this could damage the main disk, so you'd better agree to pay me dad if it all breaks down. Anyway, what yer got 'ere is what they call in the trade a salami.'

'A salami,' Susie repeated.

'Yeah . . . A salami attack, US term, it means easy amounts of money are removed in small slices over a period of time. Intention is to disguise the losses, like what Dad done at the factory. He devised their program, yer see, so he had total access. Now, if it was bigger, yer'd call it a mega salami.'

Susie stood up. 'Wait a second, I'm not with this. Is this my disk?'

Sherry shook her head. 'No. I'm explainin' what sort of thing it could be, cos it's got somethin' similar about it, but I don't wanna do nuffink wiv it yet until I got the 'ang of it all.'

Susie listened as Sherry explained what a mega salami was, how a computer hack could program into a company, one with big payrolls or funds that were transferred regularly. The hack could then reprogram the computer and direct the monies to himself, just as her father had done at the factory.

Susie began to pace up and down, then leaned across

135

Sherry. 'OK – what if it was a bank? Could it be a bank?'

Sherry agreed it could easily be a bank, and if the hacker had access to their computers then he could even divert monies to a Swiss bank account, and program the computer not to divulge the transactions until he was out of the country and the monies removed from the Swiss account.

Susie was sure she was on to it. 'Do you think your father could do something like that?'

Sherry pulled a face. 'Yeah, but he'd have to have the password, or maybe been working on their program.' She explained how all the banks and main money companies now used certain safeguards.

'Safeguards? What do you mean?'

'Well, if every hack could bang into anybody's program they'd be screwed, so they're usin' things called biometric devices, like a retina scanner. Some companies in the US 'ave got thumb print devices – amazin' things, much more advanced than over 'ere!'

Susie was trying to digest all the information, but it was difficult – she'd never even mastered the use of a simple word processor. 'OK. So say your dad had a bank password.'

Sherry giggled. 'You'd be laughin'. Hack into the electronic mailin' system.'

Susie was astonished. 'You – you can do that?'

Sherry shook her head. 'Nah! But me dad could. Once he hacked into the bank's warrant department and he was watchin' 'em buyin' and sellin' warrants.'

Susie whistled. 'Do you think that the disk I've got could have a bank's password on it?'

Sherry tapped the disk against her hand. 'Could do. I dunno. Like I said, I'm a bit wary of usin' it. See, I need a bit more time.'

Susie patted her shoulder. 'Take all the time you need. You know, you're brilliant at this, you could get a really good job.'

'Nah! Be too borin'. Me dad was in 'ere twelve hours at a time.'

Mrs Donald's disembodied voice made Susie jump. 'Sherry, dear, will you come in, please? Mrs Hazard wants to go home.'

136

Sherry switched off the computer. 'Better keep Mum 'appy, she can be such a pain.' Suddenly she frowned. 'Hazard. I know that name . . . Oh, yeah! It's Stella, right?'

Susie opened the door to go back to the house. 'Did you ever meet Mike Hazard? Apparently he used to visit your dad here.'

Sherry bit her nails. 'I dunno, Laytham was in 'ere a lot, used to drive up in his flashy Merc, and then me dad tried it on wiv me again and I just 'ad enough, so I said to Tony, I said did 'e 'ave any work goin', I was out on the street . . .'

Susie watched Sherry shut the door to the hut, and followed her down the path to the back door of the house.

'Did Laytham take you to the Rosemount Hotel by force?'

'Nah! I run off wiv 'im, but then it got all weird, and 'e started bein' as bad as me dad, knocked me around. Talk about goin' from the fryin' pan into the bleedin' fire!' She suddenly clutched hold of Susie's hand. 'His murder – I 'ad nuffink to do wiv that, honest. I was scared of him. Now if the filth find out I was there, will they come after me?'

Susie slipped her arm around Sherry's shoulders. 'Look, if they did – and they might find out you worked there – then you call me and I'll talk to them with you, OK?'

'Don't tell me mum what kind of place it was. She'll 'ave a fit!'

Stella was furious about having to sit with Mrs Donald, having to keep on looking at the face of her husband, James Donald. There seemed to be more and more photographs of him, unless it was her imagination. Her uneasiness at being there, in the dead man's house, knowing she had buried him, became greater and greater until all she wanted to do was to get out. She jumped up as Susie and Sherry came into the room. 'I'm leaving. Could I please have *my* car keys?'

Susie stood by the car as Stella carefully placed the baby in the carrycot restraint in the back seat. Another thing that

Susie hadn't paid her for or even thanked her for getting. She snatched the keys from Susie. 'Now I want that disk. I've had enough of these games. I'm going to the office and I'm going to give that thing to Al Franks. If that other brute comes, Franks can give it to him. I'm not playing these games any longer.'

Susie tried to keep her temper. 'It may look like a game to you, but it's very serious.'

'You don't have to tell me that! A man was murdered this afternoon and I've had enough. Now give me the disk!'

Susie stormed back into the house. Sherry had already gone back into the hut and was sitting by the computer, her cheeks bulging like a hamster's as she shoved in her mother's ham sandwiches. Susie joined her.

'Eh! I fink I got somethin'. I hadda thought, an' I—'

Susie looked over the desk and picked up one of the disks Sherry had been using. 'This isn't *the* one, is it?'

'No, I got it in. Look what's on the screen.'

Susie asked Sherry to wait, saying she would be back in a second. She was, and she gave Stella the disk, saying she was going to talk over a few more things with Sherry, and then she would see Stella at home. Susie hurried back down the garden as Stella drove off.

By the time Stella reached the office it was after six, and getting dark. She couldn't see any lights on, and banged the steering wheel in frustration: Susie had the office keys.

She was just about to drive off, when a dark maroon Rover drew up behind her. Stella waited, adjusting her rear-view mirror. 'Come on, move!' she muttered. The car remained directly behind her, blocking her exit. All at once she felt frightened; the car seemed ominous: no lights, just parked right across the rear of the VW.

Mike Hazard leaned up in the back seat. 'It's Stella.' He lay down again.

Alexander Reed hesitated, staring at the VW in front of him. He wore an immaculate navy blue overcoat, crisp white shirt and striped tie, with black leather driving gloves. 'Did she see you?'

Mike winced in pain, snapped that she couldn't have – and

hurry up, he had to get to a doctor soon. Reed slowly opened the car door. Watching intently in her mirror, Stella saw his grey pressed trousers, his polished black shoes as he walked towards her car. She pressed down the lock on her door, leaned over and hurriedly pressed the other side down.

Reed came right up to the window: he leaned forward and tapped lightly. 'Open the window, Mrs Hazard. Stella!'

She stared at him, terrified.

'I'm not going to hurt you. Just open the window and listen to what I have to say. I swear I won't hurt you.'

Stella was rigid. She managed to shake her head.

'I have a message from Mike, your husband, Stella. Open the window.'

With a sickening jolt, Stella recognized the panic rising inside her: she began to pant, pant, pant . . .

Reed waited a moment before lowering his head again. 'Trust me, I am a friend of Mike's. I've got a message.'

Stella opened the window, just a fraction. 'How do I know I can trust you?'

Reed moved closer, Stella could see his breath streaming out in the cold night air. 'Matt Munro, "Softly As I Leave You". He said to tell you that if you gave him the disk then he would stay dead. He knows it's not in the office, Stella, so . . . Do you have the disk?'

Stella's mouth was dry. She swallowed. Reed repeated very slowly that Mike would stay dead, then he stepped back. 'He won't come back, he's given his word. Just get the disk to me, Stella.'

She opened the glove compartment; he could see it in her hands, and he inched forward again.

Stella peered through the small aperture. 'You give him a message from me. You tell him, if he does show his face, if he even thinks of it, then so help me God I will go to the police and I will tell them everything. Here, take it!'

She threw the disk out of the window. Reed caught it and clasped it to him.

'You never saw me, Mrs Hazard, is that clear? We've never met.'

Stella kept panting, telling herself to keep control, she

139

couldn't faint now, not now. The Rover backed without turning its lights on, and moved out of the boatyard fast. So fast she couldn't have got its registration number even if she had thought of it. She did not have the faintest idea that Mike had been within yards of her and his son.

Sherry jumped up and down, then sat down again at the desk. 'It's fuckin' brilliant! This is amazin'! Do you know what this is doin'? Usin' your disk, it's gone right in an' broken the password on *eight* disks!'

Susie was just as excited. 'And? Well?'

'I dunno. I'm getting lists of numbers . . . not like a bank, maybe they're dates, or some kind of odds. It's got me lost.'

Susie looked at her watch. It was after seven and she knew Stella would be having a fit.

'I'd better go. Can you do something for me? Will you call this number? It's my portable, and what I want you to do is list all the companies you know your dad worked for, maybe devised their computer programs, OK?'

Sherry pulled a face. 'He done 'undreds – look at the files.'

Susie pulled on her coat. 'I'll pay you five pound an hour, OK?' Sherry didn't look too impressed. 'OK. Ten quid an hour then. Is it a deal?'

Sherry beamed . . . and walked with Susie down the path. She offered to babysit if ever Susie wanted, and in turn Susie promised that if ever Sherry needed her all she had to do was call.

Stella bathed, fed and changed Mike. He'd been very fussy and she took a while to get him off to sleep. Then she made herself a cup of tea, and sat down to wait. She knew she couldn't take any more, and no matter what Susie had to say about handing over the disk, Stella made up her mind that *she* was going to say what she had to say and get it off her chest, once and for all.

The front door banged. Susie yelled that she was home,

and walked into the lounge. Stella was sitting in the easy chair, smoking a cigarette.

'You been drinking again?'

'No, I have not. Now sit down, I have something to tell you – and don't you dare interrupt me, because I have tried to tell you this before, and I have just never been able to do it. Until now.'

Susie perched on the edge of the sofa.

Stella coughed, and took a deep breath. 'I went to the office. A man came up to me, before I got in, and he said he wanted the disk. I asked how I could trust him and he said—'

Susie smiled. 'That doesn't matter, Stella, because—'

'*Just listen to me!*' There was that ferociousness in her voice; her eyes were strange, almost hard. She didn't seem like the Stella Susie knew.

'He said that *if* I gave him the disk, then Mike would stay dead. He would never come back . . .'

Susie stared, not understanding – but then it hit her. She felt her heart explode.

'He's not dead, Susie. May God forgive me for what I have done. I buried the man I was asked to identify. I did it. I don't know why, or what took me over – jealousy, grief, I don't know. All I do know is that I did it, and I lied, and I've had to go on telling lies, until sometimes I wished I was dead. Mike is alive. It was Mike in that fire. He's alive, Susie.'

Susie didn't say a word. She couldn't face Stella. Every step up the stairs was leaden, she had to grip the banister rail tightly. She opened the door to the little boxroom, saw her baby sleeping – Mike's son – and gently lifted him into her arms. The tears came, heavy, awful, silent tears. Her whole body shook, but she made no sound. Mike was alive.

Stella sat in the chair, unable to cry. It was as if all the tears had been drained from her. She held a cushion to her chest, hugging it tightly as she heard Susie walking down the stairs.

She wanted to call out – but what could she say? How could she ask for forgiveness. She had told terrible lies.

Susie arrived at Mrs Donald's. She had nowhere else to go, and she apologized shamefaced, standing on the doorstep. 'There's been a bit of an emergency and . . .'

Mrs Donald insisted Susie come into the house. She wasn't in bed, she said, and Susie hadn't disturbed her at all. In fact she was waiting for Sherry who was still working outside in the garden shed.

At that moment Sherry appeared. 'You must be telepathic, I was just gonna ring ya! I got somefink. Come out an 'ave a look.'

Mrs Donald told Susie she would take care of the baby, and if she wanted to stay the night she was more than welcome.

Sherry had lists of all the companies for whom James Donald had devised programs. 'Most of 'em don't grab you, like there's a newsagent, and then there's a couple of shops and fings what he done. The bigger companies are all a possibility but, what I fink is, look . . .' Sherry jabbed the paper with her bitten fingernail. 'That could be possible! What you fink? He done a program for 'em, and then if you look at all the numbers what come up on the screen . . .'

Susie chewed her lips, she'd seen the name before. 'What is this Coomes, Sherry?'

'A chain of bettin' shops. It's a possible.'

Susie hesitated. 'You mean horse races? How did he do a program for them?'

Sherry shrugged. 'I dunno, but they must 'ave computers, like a main terminal or somefink.'

Susie nodded, her eyes flicking over the lists and lists of small companies James Donald had worked for. 'No bank, post office?'

Sherry sighed. 'Well, I've not done them files yet. Want me to start? You owe me quite a lot of dough, you know.'

Susie continued to work with Sherry for another couple of hours. It was after midnight when she put in a call to Harry

Green, after first asking Susie if she had any idea what time it was, he listened without interruption. After he had heard everything she had to say, he suggested they meet up and said that he would put the wheels in motion.

The next morning was worse than Stella could have believed possible. Alone at the breakfast table, just seeing little Mike's bowl, his bottle, and a rattle she had bought him made the loss of Susie and the baby more poignant. Stella had never felt so lonely, so empty – and yet there were no tears. It felt as if she were being punished, that she had to be punished.

The doorbell rang, and Stella's heart lifted: they'd come back. As she ran out into the hall, the phone began to ring. She didn't care about the phone, she wanted to fling her arms around Susie.

The two uniformed police officers asked if she was Mrs Stella Hazard. She nodded, dumbly. It had been stupid to think Susie would come back, that she'd let Stella care for the baby. Of course Susie would have gone to the police – she was an ex-policewoman.

'Will you wait until I get dressed?' she asked.

The officers nodded, and Stella showed them into the lounge. The phone stopped ringing, but Stella knew it wouldn't be Susie. She wondered vaguely if the officers would take her out in handcuffs – not that she knew anybody in the street, not that she even cared.

CHAPTER TEN

Susie was at Scotland Yard. She replaced the phone in her bag as Harry Green approached her. 'They just called in. She's on her way. Do you want to come up? I'll leave instructions at the desk to get her brought in.'

Susie followed Harry into the lifts. 'Have they checked into the companies I listed? One of them may be what the disk is targetted for. It's Coomes Betting Shops. What if the numbers were dates? Could be race meetings. As far as I can see there's no other company big enough for a scam of any size. Are they checking out Coomes?'

Harry gave her a sidelong look. 'They're checking all your information, Susie, but, until they can work out what's on the disk, we just have to sit tight. We can't go calling every one of those companies. If we did, we might tip off the wrong person.'

Harry looked down the list as the lift gates opened. He ushered Susie down the corridor towards the end door, through which was the Yard's computer unit's main base. Harry passed over the list of James Donald's programs to John Myers, the virus specialist, who immediately became interested in the one company Susie had ringed. Coomes Betting Shops. He polished his glasses, his eyes on his screen, then turned to his assistant. 'See if the coded numbers are dates, and check if they coincide with any race meetings coming up.'

Myers replaced his glasses. 'They may be dates. Who knows? It's a bitch. We've not had much luck so far!'

Stella was slightly fazed: the young officers were very pleasant, they didn't ask about whether or not she knew her rights, and there was no sign of handcuffs. As she saw the Scotland Yard headquarters looming, she hunched up in the back seat.

She was ushered to the reception desk, one of the officers leading her gently by the elbow. 'We have Mrs Hazard for Detective Inspector Green.'

Stella was handed a security pass name tag, and told to pin it on. Then the officer shook her hand and walked off. She stood by the reception desk, still dazed. It was all a bit strange – it certainly didn't feel like an arrest.

'Mrs Hazard?' A plain-clothes officer stepped out of the lift.

'Yes.' Stella nodded. Was he going to handcuff her, perhaps?

'Would you be kind enough to follow me, please?'

Stella stepped out of the lift just as Susie hurried out of the office right at the end of the corridor. On seeing Stella she broke into a run; she wanted to have a quiet talk with her first. Seeing Susie made Stella want to run, too: to put her arms up and around her, give her a hug. 'I'm sorry, so sorry, Susie!'

Susie looked back down the corridor, then at Stella. 'I can't talk about last night now, not now. I tried to call you, but you'd already left.'

They began to walk up the corridor.

'Is this about Laytham's murder, then?'

Susie gave a quick shake of her head. 'No, no, it's about the disk. I didn't give you the real one, that was just one from Donald's office. Don't, whatever you do, mention anything about him, or what you've done. Just listen . . .'

'Where's the baby?'

'He's safe. Sherry and her mum are looking after him.' She suddenly smiled as the tall, handsome Harry Green appeared. 'Harry, this is Stella, Stella Hazard.'

Harry shook Stella's hand. 'Glad you got here so fast. We don't have much time, and I think we're going to need you. We'll want a description of the man you gave the disk to and . . .'

They entered the office of the main Scotland Yard Computer Virus Department. Stella sat down and tried to recall what Alexander Reed looked like. She gave Harry as good a description as she could. Her heart was pounding; she had no real idea of what was going on.

Two men worked on two different computers. A printer churned out page after page of what looked like rows and rows of numbers.

Harry looked over Stella's description of Reed. 'Not a lot to go on. Do you think if you saw the man again it's possible you'd recognize him?'

'Yes, yes. I'd know him anywhere. I wouldn't forget his face!'

Harry patted her arm. 'Good. We might need you.'

His attention was drawn to Myers who let out a yell and raised his fist. 'It's coming up! I think we've cracked it!' Myers turned to his assistant. 'Feed those dates in again and see what else comes up.'

The room fell silent. Myers and his assistant seemed to communicate almost telepathically. Their screens flashed up lists of dates, numbers, dates, numbers. Those watching looked from one man to the other as they snapped out date after date, until both came up with the same one twice. An hour later, Myers removed his glasses again; he was sweating, and had to wipe his face with his handkerchief.

He stared at the screen, seeming well pleased. 'OK, we've narrowed it down. I think this must be a racing scam, and it's going to hit Coomes. There are only two big race meetings on the dates listed. One is a small local meet at Thirsk in Yorkshire, the big one is at Newmarket. That's the good news.'

Harry sucked in his breath. 'What's the bad?'

'Well, if these dates are correct, it's tomorrow. It's going down this weekend!'

Harry swore and looked at Susie. Suddenly the second virus specialist gave a yell, and stood up. 'I got it! I think I've cracked it!'

Everybody gathered around his chair, peering at his screen. Stella inched closer to Susie. 'Cracked what? I don't understand.'

Harry smiled. 'They've been working on this since six o'clock this morning. We know that James Donald worked on the computer program for a big betting chain, Coomes, and they have a central computer bank feeding their shops all over the country.'

Harry was interrupted as more data came up onto the screen. Myers clapped his hands. 'It's amazing! The disk has all their private clients' account numbers. I think – I'm still not one hundred per cent sure – but there must be a hell of a lot of people involved. I reckon the scam centres on insider knowledge of a sure-fire winner, maybe one with low odds. Someone will have to be connected to Coomes to place the disk into their main terminal. The bets go down on the dead cert, and I reckon, though I can't be completely certain yet, that when the massive bets come in on accounts, the program holds the odds down – as far as I can see it won't register them on all the shops' screens, so it doesn't give anything away. Then the horse romps home and into any one of these accounts – or into God knows how many – goes the winnings.'

A row of confused faces stared back at Myers. He attempted to explain it further. 'OK, say you place thirty grand on a horse at thirty-three to one, nice earner, and if – and we're still not certain – if the account, because of the virus command, drains all the other accounts, somebody is looking at a massive pay-off. It's so complicated that until I've had more time I still can't be sure how it will work – and as the meet goes down tomorrow, I don't have much time.'

Harry rubbed his chin. 'But it's Newmarket, and it's this weekend, yes? Is there any way you can come up with which race?'

Myers rubbed his eyes. 'Nope, but somebody inside Coomes has got to be in on the scam, because he will have to insert this disk into their main terminal.'

Stella whispered to Susie, 'But you said you gave me the wrong one, so it can't work, can it?'

Harry overheard and rested his hand on Susie's shoulder. 'It's always tough to prove a fraud, because we're always brought in *after* the event. By that time the fraud has been executed and the perpetrators could be anywhere – Rio,

Canada, you name it. We know this scam can't work, because they don't have this disk, but a fraud is going to be attempted – a massive one – and we're in on it before it's due to go down.'

Myers continued to work. Then he stared at his screen again. 'I would say the bloke that devised this would, no doubt, also have devised some means of covering his tracks, so that when the fraud was completed, the virus would scramble who got what pay-out etcetera. You see, it has every single account number attached to the betting shops. There's thousands of them, all over the country.'

Superintendent Jellings walked in, a tall, dark-haired man, very tense. Harry introduced Stella and Susie. Jellings was curt, almost dismissive, as he stood by Myers's desk.

'Right, any development?'

Myers started again. 'Well, sir, the disk is programmed to log into the mainframe, and then it runs a rogue change in the accounting software, so when their horse – which is probably a dead cert runner – one of maybe dozens of possible credit card punters gets a bonanza win into their bank account, for example. You with me?'

A row of blank faces stared back, now with one extra as even Jellings was having a hard time trying to absorb it all. He was obviously impatient, not interested in the virus and its complexity – he simply required the criminal fraudsters to be identified.

Harry Green didn't want to lose Jellings's backing, so he tried another tactic. 'We can't pinpoint who's involved unless we start going through every single account, every name. It'd take days. We don't even know which race. All we do know is it's Newmarket, and this weekend. Our best bet – sorry about the pun, sir – is if we first check on all Coomes employees, to see if there's anyone with a connection to James Donald.'

Jellings nodded and checked his watch. 'Well, get started. Anything else?'

Harry ushered Stella forward. 'Mrs Hazard passed over a disk to a man who assumed it was the real McCoy. She believes she could recognize him again.'

148

Jellings pulled at his ear. 'Mmm, so the fraud itself cannot actually be pulled off?'

Harry nodded. 'No, but it's a chance it could go again. I mean, we don't have this guy Donald. We think he must have started the blaze at the factory where these disks are or were made. He himself was at one time employed by the same factory. Two men died, sir. Donald was badly burned in the fire, and taken to Richmond burns unit. He skipped before he could be questioned, so it's not just a fraud.'

Jellings pursed his lips. 'OK, let's move on it as fast as we can, see if we can get some more information. And I'll talk to the chief. Good work!'

Harry Green thanked Jellings. Susie and Stella looked at one another: nobody seemed interested in their role, especially not Jellings.

Stella and Susie sat together in the canteen. They had still not talked about the previous evening, and neither of them wanted to bring up the subject. Stella was unusually silent, almost scared to say anything that would make waves. In some ways she was relieved just to be with Susie.

'We have to play this pretty close to the chest, Stella, make no mention of what we know about Donald – especially Mike's part in it all. Understand?'

Stella nodded. There was a lot she wanted to ask, but she just kept quiet. Susie went to check if the baby was all right, calling Mrs Donald from a phone box. Mike was perfectly happy, Mrs Donald assured her, there was nothing to worry about. He was in very capable hands, she had been a nursery teacher and a baby minder, and would, if Susie had allowed her, have continued to chat about her past life and how many children she had known, and if ever Susie wanted someone to take care of Mike all she had to do was call. 'Thank you, Mrs Donald, I really do appreciate your kindness. I'll call again soon.'

Susie felt that pang again. She touched the phone, almost wanting to call Mrs Donald again, but she told herself that was silly, and she would only get another lengthy anecdote

149

about Mrs Donald's ability with children, so she went back to Stella. Stella made her give a blow-by-blow account of every single word Mrs Donald had said, and was as bad if not worse than Mrs Donald. 'Stella, Mike is fine, Mrs Donald just told me he was asleep, and that she was also very capable of looking after him because she worked as a baby minder. I'm not as bad a mother as you keep harping on at me about. Mike is fine.'

Stella seemed very tart. 'Well, she can have him while we're here, but, I mean, you mustn't make this a habit, it's not good for him to be moved around, you know. If you give me the number I'll keep calling just to check.'

Susie sighed. 'Stella, Mike is perfectly well, and I will call, on the hour every hour, now are you satisfied?'

'We'd best do it around his feed-time, so if he's asleep it won't wake him when the phone rings.'

Susie smiled, it was so obvious that Stella loved Mike, almost as if he were her own son. In a funny way, maybe, part of him was, and Susie felt more love for Stella than she would or could have believed possible, especially after what she had done.

Lunchtime. By now Harry Green and his team had talked with Coomes and listed every single employee with access to the firm's main computer terminal. None of them, so far as they could ascertain, had had any contact with James Donald. Most employees with direct access had worked for Coomes for a number of years, and all were considered trustworthy.

Harry was disappointed, but the manager of Coomes agreed to give him access to his office. A window with venetian blinds opened onto the main floor of the office. Stella was to be taken in the back way: it was obviously imperative that if the man to whom she passed the disk did work in the office, he should not see her and be alerted to the possible danger of detection.

She sat in the office until three o'clock. She saw every man who worked at Coomes, but, and she was very positive, she did not recognize any of them as being Alexander Reed, the man to whom she gave the disk.

Once again, Harry was disappointed, worried that Jellings might pull the case. He asked for two officers to be placed inside Coomes to keep a watch on the employees. But by four thirty in the afternoon that was all he had got. Again he pressed Jellings for a full-scale surveillance operation to take place on the racecourse itself, emphasizing Stella's part in being able to identify at least one member of the scam ring.

At five o'clock, following meetings with the Newmarket stewards and the local police, Jellings gave the go-ahead. 'Operation Newmarket' would be given fifteen officers and a fully equipped surveillance van, the type used for controlling football crowds, complete with screens linked to cameras positioned around the racecourse. The stands, the enclosures, all would be monitored. The police knew the scam could not work: their job was to find out who was behind it.

The officers inside Coomes's main computer terminal office had instructions to report directly to the surveillance truck if they saw any employee attempting to insert a disk into the main terminal.

The costs of the operation were mounting. Jellings took Harry Green aside. He was getting slightly hot under the collar and wanted to be sure that Mrs Hazard would be co-operative. She was their only eye witness: could she still be certain she would recognize the man to whom she gave the disk? Harry confirmed his confidence in Mrs Hazard.

Susie asked Stella again. 'You sure now, Stella? Sure you'd recognize him?' They were back in the canteen and it was after six.

Stella had been asked the same question, over and over again, all day. 'Yes, yes, I am sure! He scared the life out of me, and I'd never forget his voice. He said that Mike would stay dead, stay away for good if I handed it over. Do you think I'd forget that? Forget him?'

Susie gave Stella's hand a squeeze. 'OK, it's OK. Now, I assume they're going to mike you up?'

Stella gaped. 'What?'

'They'll give you a microphone, plus an officer, plain

151

clothes. He'll be at your side. Anything you say will be recorded back in the surveillance truck. If you do see this bloke, all you do is mark him, describe what he's wearing, and they'll do the rest.'

Stella panted. 'Right. Do they know which race it is yet?'

Susie shook her head. 'They don't know which race, which horse, or who's betting.'

'Well, they've not got a lot to go on then, have they?'

'They've got you, Stella, and Harry's pulling out all the stops.'

Stella breathed in deeply. 'I noticed. He seems to think he's a real Perry Mason. Has he thanked you at all? I mean, all the work you've been doing, and me too. They wouldn't have anything if it wasn't for you and me.'

Harry walked into the canteen and called over, asking if they wanted another cup of tea.

Stella drained her cup. 'They do a lot of this, don't they? I've never had so many cups of tea, not even at the bread shop – but, yes, I'll have another. And I'll have one of those buns with the pink icing.'

Susie joined Harry at the canteen counter. He gave a sidelong glance at Stella. 'You *sure* she'll recognize this bloke? Only we've not got a lot to go on. And I suppose you've noticed Jellings is like a jelly. It's costing a fortune, this surveillance.'

Susie chose a large, sticky pink iced bun. 'She'll do it. She's not as dizzy as she looks. Believe me, I know.'

Harry carried the tray over to the table and set it down. 'We'll be leaving in about half an hour. Anything you need will be provided. You're booked into a first class hotel, there's even a small dress shop attached to it, and we've arranged for it to stay open, so anything you require for tomorrow will be on us.'

The bun was half-way to Stella's mouth. 'Where are we going?'

Harry looked at Susie, then back to Stella. 'Newmarket, Mrs Hazard. The races are on tomorrow, we've got a lot of things to set up.'

Stella couldn't take so much as a mouthful. She was sure

there would be someone else she would see at the races. Mike. Mike Hazard.

CHAPTER ELEVEN

The police were dotted around the train. Jellings sat with Harry Green. As prearranged they made no contact with Stella and Susie, who were to get a taxi from the station directly to the hotel. The room was booked, and a shop assistant waiting for them. It was dark, almost eight thirty, as the two sat opposite each other in the first class compartment.

'So I'll have a microphone taped up to me, then?' she asked.

'Yes, and if you feel dizzy or faint, just pant. Any problem whatsoever and they'll be listening in.'

Stella licked her lips. 'Right. Won't you be with me?'

'Yes, of course, but in the surveillance van.'

'Why not on the racecourse?'

'I might stick out, Stella, you know? I'm not exactly the green wellie type. OK, this is it, we're here.'

Stella was first off the train. She looked back to see if Jellings and Harry were close, and Susie dug her in the back. 'Just walk on – you never know if somebody is watching us. You can identify him, what if he can recognize *you*? So keep your eyes peeled, he could even be on the train.'

As Stella walked on she could feel the sweat trickling down from her armpits, and just as they reached the ticket barrier, a man barged past and almost gave her heart failure. For a few moments she lost sight of Susie as she went through the barrier.

Susie gave the man a good glare, the rude bastard, then moved on, hurrying to catch up with Stella. They needed a taxi.

Kenny Graham froze. He'd seen Susie, seen her looking for Stella, and he waited until she was well past the ticket collector before he followed.

*

Stella was seated in the taxi, Susie getting in beside her. Kenny caught just a quick glimpse; he still had not seen Stella. He had to wait for a free taxi and, pushing the next couple in line out of the way, he yanked open the door.

'Tenner for you, mate. See that cab just moving out the station? Keep on its arse, will you?'

They arrived at the five star Majestic Hotel, and Stella pulled her old windcheater close. 'I'm a bit under-dressed. This place looks very posh.'

Susie was paying the taxi driver. 'Just go in and get our keys. We've got to get you all togged up.'

Stella made a very embarrassed entrance into the hotel foyer while Susie waited for change from the driver.

Kenny's cab pulled up at the kerbside. He'd been right. It was her. It was that black bitch. Hazard's wife!

Rodney Millbank's stud farm was a massive, sprawling estate with stables and yards, glorious gardens and an old manor house. The farm was situated fifteen miles from Newmarket. That night the forecourt was filled with an array of expensive motors, the house was blazing with lights, the cocktail party in full swing. Music drifted across the courtyard, the low, muted sound of laughter and people talking as the well-heeled guests arrived.

The stable complex had living quarters for the stable lads, jockeys and trainers. There were eighteen horse boxes, their occupants already bedded down for the night.

Mike Hazard was in one of the stable lads' rooms, a small flatlet above a stable. He had been checked over by a doctor friend of Reed's, had his hands and chest rebandaged and the wounds to his face were still dark and crusted. He continued to suffer a great deal of pain, and had slept very little. The discomfort in his chest was excruciating; smoke inhalation had left him with rasping breath.

Reed passed him a glass of brandy, which he cupped in his thickly bandaged hands.

'You know you're seven grand short.'

Mike sighed. 'So deduct it from my take.'

Reed shrugged. 'He won't like it. He wanted it all tonight.'
He stared at Mike. 'You can't stay here after tomorrow. If
the Gov'nor knew you were up here, he'd pull out.'

'Don't tell him then!' snapped Mike.

Reed adjusted his bow-tie and pulled at his evening suit.
'Why you had to get involved with those low life . . .'

Mike sipped the brandy, and leaned back. 'Without the
low life, Alex my old son, you'd have nothing. Without me,
you'd have fuck all!'

Reed stared at Hazard. 'What about Laytham?'

'What about him? He's dead. Like you said, he was low
life so nobody's gonna miss him, right? They beat up my wife,
for chrissakes, she was pregnant. You think I'd just take that?'

Reed lit a cigar. 'Kenny's late. He was supposed to be here
an hour ago so you'd better control him. This has all got out
of hand – you know, if the boss got so much as a whiff of
what's been going on he wouldn't go through with it.'

Mike said, 'Well, don't tell him. Enjoying his party, are
you? I'm surprised he lets second class citizens like you mingle
with his friends.' He stared hard at Reed. 'Come on, Alex,
calm down, we're almost there. I'll be out of the country this
time tomorrow. Your debts paid off, Millbank happy – we'll
all be rich men. Just stay calm.'

The stable door banged and Reed jumped. Mike laughed.
'Go and put a few drinks down you. You're making me
nervous.'

Kenny Graham wove around the Mercs, Land-rovers, Range-
rovers and Saabs. He looked towards the manor house and
spat. He continued round to the stable area, hearing the sound
of horses' hoofs as he turned a corner. Wee Georgie, one of
Millbank's trainers, was pushing and shoving a massive chest-
nut which was playing up.

'Eh! That Julianna, Georgie?' Kenny grinned.

Georgie looked. 'No, you prat. This is a gelding, an' a right
bastard. I've just had to segregate him, he's a bloody nuisance,

156

freaks out at anythin' – and if you had any nonce, you'd see this was a fuckin' gelding. This is Roman. Our girl's in the end stall. Julianna.'

Kenny backed away from Roman, as Georgie pulled at his bit. 'Back up, you bugger! Go on!'

'Eh, Georgie, will our girl do it tomorrow?'

Georgie snorted. 'What am I? She's been running long distance all season, but she's a sprinter! She'll go like a bullet, I'd put my life on it!'

Kenny laughed. 'If she don't do that, Georgie, your life might just be on it!'

Hearing Kenny's voice, Reed shut Hazard's door and hurried downstairs from the stables to the yard. He was suddenly more confident. Mike was right: this time tomorrow he would be a rich man, most of it already owing, and he had no intention of clearing out. This was his life . . .

Kenny raced up to him. 'We got a problem. She was on the train, that black bitch, Hazard's wife! She's an ex-cop, isn't she? So what's she doing here?'

Reed put his fingers to his lips, gestured for Kenny to go back down to the yard. He looked towards the bedroom, listened, then followed Kenny. They went into the tack room.

'Hazard's here, he's up in the stables, and—' Reed chucked Mike's holdall '—he's seven grand short.'

Kenny clenched his hands. 'He killed Laytham, he fucking smashed his head in. Cops been swarming all over the place, I'll fucking kill him!'

Reed shut the door. 'Wait! Just wait. He can't move, he's still all burnt up. What was that about his wife?'

Mike inched out of bed. He heard every word Kenny had said. He made it to the yard. The music from the house was louder out here and he couldn't be sure where Reed and Kenny were. Then he saw the lights on in the tack room.

★

Reed covered his face. This was crazy, he didn't know what he should do. 'You shouldn't have beaten up his wife!'

Kenny pushed at Reed. 'Don't you fuckin' tell me what to do! Laytham was my friend, I'm not just gonna take that, take what he done to him and not do anything about it. I'll fucking wring his neck!'

Reed brushed his sleeve down where Kenny had grabbed him. 'You will do nothing unless I say so. One word to Millbank, the whole thing's off.'

'What about Hazard's wife? I don't trust him, I don't trust her, she was a cop just like him. She's at the bleeding Majestic Hotel. How did she know to come here? She knows, I'm tellin' you, she knows.'

Reed opened a drawer, hands shaking. He carefully removed a stun-gun used to drug the horses. 'Here, take this. Use it on her, but watch out you don't kill her, and then . . . if need be, you sort out Hazard. But not until the meet is over.'

Kenny laughed as he snapped the gun case closed. 'I'll be right back, OK?'

Reed nodded. He felt terrible, disgusted at himself – he was no better or worse than Kenny. 'I'll go back up to the house, tell Millbank everything's on schedule. He'll want the cash – not now, later, bring it up to the house later, when everybody's gone, and for chrissakes don't mention any of this . . . Use my car.' He tossed over his keys. Kenny caught them in his big fist.

Reed walked out of the tack room, and crossed the stableyard heading back to the manor house. Kenny waited, then after a while he walked out carrying the gun case. He went to Reed's Volvo and got in, placing the gun case on the seat beside him.

He started up the engine and drove out, past all the guests' cars, and turned into the dark lane outside the manor's main gates.

He had driven quite a distance when he suddenly became aware that someone was in the car with him. He flicked a look into the driving mirror. Mike Hazard sat in the back seat, smiling, and now Kenny had something that felt like a gun pressed into the back of his neck.

'Just keep on driving, Kenny, nice and steady, until I tell you when to stop.'

Mike reached over and picked up the gun case . . .

Stella had hung up the new suit and blouse, and laid out the new shoes and underwear. She was wearing a hotel courtesy towelling robe. 'I'm not sure about the hat. What do you think about it?'

Susie inspected the large-brimmed navy and pink hat. That part was all right – it was the large blue feather she was unsure of. 'We won't be able to miss you, that's for sure!'

Stella placed the hat on her head, and studied herself in the mirror. The price tag swung in front of her eyes. She took the hat off and gasped, 'My God, this hat! Do you know how much it cost? Two hundred and twenty-two pounds! Susie, this hat cost . . .'

Susie grinned. 'We're not paying, so why worry? Did you get some rollers and shampoo?'

Stella nodded. 'Yes, and I got some earrings and—'

Susie passed over a menu. 'Choose what you want and I'll order room service.'

They sat facing each other, dining in the suite with a good bottle of wine. At last Susie spoke about Mike. She had made up her mind that if, as she suspected, they should see him at the races, Stella was to act crazy. They could get over the fact that she had wrongly identified James Donald – cover it up by saying she was in deep shock. So if Stella saw Mike she was to act crazy, even faint if she felt like it.

'I won't need to act, Susie . . . but they'll arrest him!'

Susie nodded. 'Yes. He'll be arrested.'

'Can you – I mean, would you . . . want that?'

Susie didn't hesitate. 'Yes, Mike will be arrested, he should

159

have been a long time ago, Stella. I never wanted to believe all the stories about him, maybe I just refused to believe them, then when I got pregnant I just guess I put blinkers on, like one of those horses we're gonna see. Well, the blinkers are off. And if Mike is at that racecourse, *I* will – if you don't – tip them off to pick him up. It's the only way, then we'll be free of him, he'll be out of our lives.'

Stella nodded, impressed by Susie, by her calmness, and she reached over to touch her hand. 'You know, I admire you and, well, if you can do it, so can I. So – cheers!'

Susie lifted her glass. 'Good luck for tomorrow!'

Colin Jenkins couldn't sleep. He was the Coomes betting shop link, the man they depended upon to insert the virus disk into the Coomes main computer terminal. He was scared. He had even taken one of his mother's sleeping tablets, but nothing could put his mind at rest. He had half hoped they wouldn't go through with it. Now he had no choice. The disk was on his dressing table where it seemed almost to glow. Jenkins started sweating, tossing and turning again. He'd always known that Mike Hazard would pull in the favour – one day. He had not reckoned that the price would be so high. Mike Hazard had got him off a little bit of receiving back in the early eighties. He had checked out the small hardware store Jenkins ran, and found a number of television sets and car radios. Kids, Jenkins had explained, they just kept on bringing the stuff, and wouldn't take no for an answer. Hazard had spent a long time checking out the stolen goods and then shrugged: it was too much aggravation to get all the paperwork done. He'd taken a good car stereo and a few other things, and walked out, pausing at the door to wag his finger at Jenkins. 'You owe me, remember that!' Jenkins had gone straight ever since. He sold the business and found a good job in one of the smaller betting shops. Then he had started work for Coomes. As soon as he had seen Mike Hazard again, he had known that he would want something from him. He had been right. Mike had given hardly any sign that he recognized

Jenkins. He'd placed and bet and walked out. He returned three or four times, and never gave Jenkins more than a cursory glance, but then one afternoon after Jenkins had finished work Mike had appeared in his car, and offered Jenkins a lift home. It had seemed innocent enough. Mike was smiling and chatting about the weather, so nothing had really prepared Jenkins for the moment when Mike had stopped the car, and rested his hand across Jenkins's shoulder. 'I'm glad things have worked out for you, Colin. Could all have been very different, eh? Bit of time away, and you would never have got yourself this nice cushy job.'

Thinking that Mike was going to touch him for a few quid, Jenkins had reached for his wallet. 'No, no, come on, Colin. I'm not hitting you for cash. What you think I am, eh?'

Colin had replaced his wallet, but Mike's arm remained along the back of the seat. 'I need a favour though, Colin, and of course you'll be paid for it. Some friends of mine want you to do something for them.'

Jenkins chewed his lips. 'Look, Mike, I know I owe you—'

'Yes, well, that's good, always good to repay a debt, isn't it, Colin? Let me tell you, it's so simple, and, like I said, you will be paid a lot of money. It was your lucky day when I came into the shop. I mean, I didn't even know you worked there, so it's lucky for you, lucky for me . . .'

Jenkins asked hesitantly what Mike wanted. When he told him, he almost wet himself with nerves. The hand gripped his neck hard, making him even more afraid. 'Now, listen, all you will have to do is, on a certain date, insert a disk into the main terminal, OK? You can remove it as soon as the program goes through, so nobody will know who did it, nobody will find out . . . Fifteen grand, Colin.'

When poor Jenkins had stuttered out that he would never be able to do it, Mike had slapped his head hard. 'I went out on a limb for you. Now you don't back down on me or, so help me God, I'll have you picked up for that bit of thieving I got you off! *Understand?*'

They had met again only once. With Hazard had been a man referred to as Reed, no Christian name. After Reed had left, Hazard quietly told Jenkins that the money would be delivered to his home, and if he ever even thought of a double cross he would be a very sorry, silly little man.

Jenkins had agreed, and waited. When nobody showed, when nobody, not even Mike Hazard, came to the shop again, he had thought he was safe; the plan wasn't going ahead. Then a courier arrived at his home with an envelope containing the small disk, and instructions as to exactly what time he was to insert it into the computer. Nothing else. The phone call came later, not from Hazard, but from someone he didn't know, a soft well-spoken voice which simply said that he had better do what he had been asked, and if he didn't they would know. Colin Jenkins didn't say a word, but waited until the caller had hung up before he replaced the phone.

His hand was shaking now as he brewed up a cup of tea. Hearing a creaking noise, he glanced up at the ceiling and winced. Had he woken her?

'Is that you, Colin?' his mother called out.

He sighed, and fetched another cup and saucer. He carried some tea carefully upstairs and entered his mother's bedroom. She was sitting up, her shawl wrapped around her thin shoulders. 'Can't you sleep, dear?'

'No, no, I'm a bit restless.' He placed the cup on her bedside table, then plumped up her pillows.

'Oh dear, and you've got a busy weekend. You must get a good night's rest. You've been looking very peaky lately.'

Jenkins fetched the bottle of Mogadon. 'Just a bit under the weather, Ma, no need to worry.'

She smiled as she sipped her tea. 'Well, I do – and you need a holiday. If they paid you better, we could go on a cruise. I dream of being taken on a cruise, it would be so nice, just you and me.'

He smiled softly: they'd be able to go on a cruise all right after tomorrow – in fact, they could stay on one for the rest of their lives. The thought suddenly made him feel better, more positive. He leaned over his beloved mother and kissed her wrinkled cheek. 'Yeah, a cruise would be real nice and, well, you never know, one of these days we might just be able to take one . . .'

She smiled into his thin waspish face. 'Oh, that would be lovely, Colin, I've always fancied going to Bermuda.'

The following morning Jenkins shaved, dressed and carried his mother's breakfast up to her; then, having made sure she had everything she would need until lunchtime, he locked the front door behind him and walked briskly down the road to catch his bus.

The disk was in his jacket pocket; he kept patting it to reassure himself it was still there. The bus was late, and he stared at the posters in the bus shelter: 'Sand and Sea Cruises' advertized their 'fabulous summer breaks!' Colin Jenkins smiled. It was a good omen. On the bus he opened his paper, and turned to the racing section. He looked down the runners at Newmarket, and glanced at the second race of the meeting. Julianna, owned by Rodney Millbank, trained by Alexander Reed. Jenkins suddenly realized who Reed was, but it was too late to do anything. Besides, he was looking forward to that cruise. How the scam was to work he didn't know and didn't care.

CHAPTER TWELVE

Stella flushed the toilet, and scuttled out into the hotel bedroom. It was the sixth time she had been – she put it down to all the tea she had drunk the previous day, but it was nerves. Susie was getting her coat on as Stella straightened her skirt.

'You sure you're all right?'

'I'm fine, it's just all that tea – then the wine last night. I'm glad they don't have the microphone on me now, though. All that flushing would give them earache!'

Susie laughed and looked on as Stella batted her mascara'd eyelashes as she posed with the hat on. 'What do you think?'

'You look great, very county, dah-ling – but you should have got flat shoes, you'll be walking all round the course!'

Stella looked down at the high heels. 'I never thought! Should I change them?'

Susie checked her watch. 'You don't have time, they'll be picking you up any minute now. I'd better be going. There's an officer coming up to see you, he'll fix the microphone. Stella?'

Stella was back in the toilet again. Susie waited, checking her watch. Harry was picking her up outside the hotel at nine thirty. She was getting a bit edgy about leaving Stella on her own until the officer came. 'Don't open the door to anyone but DI Stokes – Barry Stokes. Do you hear me?'

The lavatory flushed once more and Stella emerged, her cheeks bright pink. 'Yes, Barry Stokes. He'll come to the room. I know, you've told me and all I do is keep looking for the man.'

'That's right. And if you do see him, back off fast. Don't tip him off!'

'I won't, besides he'd never recognize me in this rig out, it cost more than six months' salary at the Bake O Bread . . . Gawd! If Beryl could see me now!'

Susie checked her watch yet again. 'I'm off – and, Stella, if Mike—'

Stella interrupted, 'I know, I know. Act crazy, scream. I *know*. Well, good luck, and you'd best be going.'

Susie gave Stella a wink, then went over and kissed her cheek. 'Good luck!'

As the door shut behind Susie, Stella shot back into the toilet: nerves always affected her bladder, always had done, she'd had a terrible time at her own wedding . . . Her dad began to think she'd never make it up the aisle without having to go.

She brushed down her skirt and straightened her jacket. How strange – of all the times to be thinking about her wedding day, now, when she might be the one to instigate Mike's arrest. She sat down on the bed. Was that really the last time she'd had nerves like this? Had her life really been so devoid of any excitement that . . . ?

Someone tapped softly at the door. Stella stood up and took a deep breath. She fetched her handbag and hat, and crossed to the door. 'Come in. I'd best fix my hat—'

As Stella opened the door, Mike Hazard stepped inside. He moved fast, placing his hand over her mouth. 'Don't scream. Please don't scream, Stella, it's me, it's Mike.'

Mike kicked the door shut. Stella pulled away from him and, colliding with the bed, sat down abruptly. 'Mike!'

As Mike turned, he pulled the sweater neck away from his face. Stella saw the terrible mess it was in, one side of it red raw and scabbed. His hands were encased in hideous heavy burns gloves, just the tips of his fingers showing. He dropped the bag with the money onto the carpet beside him.

'Stella . . . I thought – I thought it was Susie. I thought Susie and the baby were here.'

Stella stared. 'Oh, did you? Well, I'm sorry to disappoint you, but it's me. It's me – Stella. Your wife.'

Mike shook his head. 'I'm sorry.'

'You're sorry? *You are sorry?*'

165

Mike sighed. 'Yes, I never meant to drag you into all this, but I got in deeper and deeper.'

Stella glared at him. 'You were always in it, and I was too stupid to see it, see that you – you were always no good! But don't apologize to me, don't beg me to forgive you for what you've put me through! You bastard! You just wanted to see Susie, did you? You just wanted to see her and your son. What about me, Mike? Don't I matter?'

'You know I always loved you, Stella, I would never have left you broke. I was never going to walk away and leave you with nothing.'

'You liar! You sicken me, *you liar*!'

She swung out at him and Mike stepped aside, holding his hands up. 'Mind my face.'

The officer pulled over in the patrol car. The man was in a ditch by the side of a field. He could have lain there for days unnoticed, but a farmer and two of his lads with a tractor wanted to open the gates. They were all gathered round the man, who looked as if he were in a deep sleep.

The officer bent down and shook Kenny Graham's arm, but he made no response. He tested his neck, feeling for a pulse. There appeared to be no sign of violence. The man was reasonably well dressed, he did not smell of liquor, but his pulse was very low. An ambulance was called. By the time it arrived Kenny Graham was dead. They had discovered his identity by means of his wallet, but as to the cause of death, that they would not know for many hours. The veterinary stun pellets, the horse drug, had killed him.

Mike couldn't believe Stella. She repeated that he should get out fast, that Susie was at the racecourse and would have him arrested.

'You're kidding, Stella!'

'Then you go to the track. She knows about you, Mike, she knows everything – even that I buried someone else. We have no secrets.'

'They'll arrest you too, Stella.' Mike cocked his head to one side. 'You'll be done for fraud. So let's stop playing games. I need help to get away, I need a new passport.'

He unzipped the money bag, and Stella watched as he displayed the cash. 'This can still work, we can all be rich. I'll split it with you.'

'I don't want your filthy money! I just want rid of you – just get out, and make it fast, because any moment there's a police officer coming up to meet me.'

He laughed. 'Oh, yes, I'm convinced! Now go and order a car, they got a Hertz desk here.'

The telephone rang and Stella snatched it up. 'This is the police, Mike. You'd better believe me – because one word from me and they'll be up here.'

Although Mike could not hear, the caller was DI Barry Stokes, who was waiting for Stella in reception. 'Mrs Hazard? This is Barry Stokes, I am in—'

Mike pressed the phone off. 'You always were a lousy liar, Stella. Now, you'd better do as I say . . .'

He delved into the bag, and withdrew the gun, the same one he'd used to kill Kenny Graham. Stella gasped, backing away from the phone. 'Oh, my God. You would use that on me . . .'

'I need a car, Stella, I need help. You'd better do it, now.'

The door was rapped hard. 'Mrs Hazard! Are you all right? This is DI Stokes. Mrs Hazard?'

Mike freaked. He looked to Stella, then to the closed door. He hadn't locked it.

Stella made a grab for the money bag, hugging it to her. 'I've change my mind. I'm having this.'

Mike looked at the door again as DI Stokes knocked louder. 'Please don't let them pick me up, please don't let them put me away, Stella. I'll – I'll leave you—'

Stella called out to DI Stokes that she was just coming. She edged closer to the door, still clasping the money case. 'I want your word, Mike, that you will never come back, never show your face again. I want you to swear on your son's life.' She called out louder, 'The door isn't locked, come in!'

Mike looked terrified: she had never seen that look on his

face before. Stella took out two stacks of banknotes. 'I want your word, your promise – and you can go out through the bathroom.'

Mike promised, his hands held out in front of him, pleadingly. He looked sick, he looked pitiful – and Stella positively enjoyed throwing the money down on the floor, watching him scrabble for it before bolting like a rabbit into the bathroom, just as DI Stokes walked in.

'Ah! Sorry to keep you waiting. Now I've got a few things here I'd like put in the hotel safe.' Stella smiled, as the bathroom door quietly closed.

Colin Jenkins hung up his jacket, and went into the small kitchen area used by the employees of Coomes main betting shop for making tea and coffee. The manager was in there, tea already brewing. 'There'll be a couple of blokes from Hammersmith here, Colin, just helping out. Could be a rushed weekend!'

Jenkins poured a cuppa into his own mug. There was nothing to alert him that anything out of the ordinary was happening. The manager often called in extra people to cope with the workload when a big race meeting was on. As he lifted the mug to his lips he was aware of the disk in his pocket. He shot a look at the wall clock: he had plenty of time, the first race wasn't even running yet. Just so long as he put it into the main terminal before two o'clock. There was plenty of time . . . He knew the instructions off by heart. He looked up at the board where the runners were listed. Millbank's horse, Julianna, was there, no odds chalked up as yet. As he went about his usual business, Colin moved closer and closer to the main terminal, the disk in his pocket, calculating just how and when he would be able to insert it safely into the computer.

Susie sat in the surveillance truck. There were eight screens all showing different views of the course; the stands, the rails, the paddocks, the winning enclosure. The crowds were just beginning to build.

'She's wearing a very distinctive hat – pink and navy blue straw, with a big feather . . .'

No one seemed too interested: they were busy setting up, running through the tests on their wires, spotting the local men and so on. Jellings was having all runners in the afternoon's five big races checked out. The stewards were double-checking that no horse was substituted. Everything was being done as unobtrusively as possible. Details of owners, trainers and runners were being fed into the truck but so far there was nothing of note to raise suspicions: everyone appeared to be legitimate. The mass of detail and names was considerable, however, and it was a slow process – which they were fully aware they would not be able to complete before the meet began.

Now the crowds were swelling, the bookies setting up their stands. The members' enclosure was filling as the stands and private boxes suddenly came to life. Susie peered closer at one screen up by the main gates.

'Stella's just arrived,' an officer reported, as he listened in to radio feedback. Susie pointed to the screen. Stella was visible, being ushered forward to the rails by Stokes. They could relay messages to him, and every word Stella said could be heard, but she could not contact them direct.

'There she is! They're going towards the rails.' Susie pointed Stella out – and Jellings laughed at her hat. Everyone was listening and watching closely, checking and double-checking. The horses were being led out from the paddock for the first race . . .

Stella's high heels dug deep into the grass and she was glad of Stokes's steady hand on her elbow as she kept tripping up and getting stuck.

'Just keep your eyes peeled, Mrs Hazard, clock the faces. We'll keep on the move and if you spot our man, just tell me.'

Stella nodded, but the crowds were getting thicker and

169

thicker, faces blurred into one. She began to doubt if she really could spot the man now. Staggering in the grass didn't help.

Coomes was a hive of activity as races all round the country were being fed into the computers. Loudspeakers kept up a running commentary of the horse *and* dog races. Now the odds were being listed and it was time for Jenkins to insert the disk. He passed Mavis who was working at the main terminal, feeding in data, and leaned over the back of her chair, as if to check the screen. 'You want to grab a quick break now, Mavis, before they line up? I'll take over here.'

Mavis thanked him, and pushed her chair back. He sat down, checking the screen. He gave a quick, furtive glance around and slowly withdrew the disk from his inside pocket. DI Stanley looked up as Mavis passed him, and turned back towards her desk, just as Jenkins eased out the disk. Stanley straightened, passed his mate and nodded. They walked casually towards Jenkins, apparently more interested in the main screens lining the walls than anything else. 'Small, sandy-haired bloke. He's at the main terminal now . . . Can we have an ID? It was a woman working there two seconds ago.'

The area manager hurried towards DI Stanley. The man was Colin Jenkins, the under manager, he whispered.

Stanley ran his eyes down the list provided by the company and turned to his mate. 'He's listed as having access to the main terminal. You got a clear view of him? What's he doing? Can you see? His shoulder's in my way. Can you see him?'

'He's got a disk . . . Shit! He's putting it in the terminal!'

The small disk was half in and half out, as Stanley grabbed Jenkins's wrist. Jenkins felt as if his heart was bursting with terror. He whipped round, his face glistening with sweat. All he said was, 'No, no, please, no, please, Mike Hazard, it was Mike Hazard . . .'

Harry Green listened intently, then he tapped Jellings's shoulder. 'We got our inside man. Name's Colin Jenkins. He's the under manager. That's the good news. The bad news is . . . the stupid bastard's nabbed him too fast, the disk wasn't actually inside the computer. He's sayin' it was a mistake!'

Jellings grabbed the phone, as Harry switched it to speaker. 'Was he putting it in or not, for chrissakes?'

Harry looked at Susie. She leaned closer. 'You know there's nothing on that disk. I mean, it's more important we get him to give us the names of who he worked for.'

Harry took Susie aside. 'He did. He said he was only approached by one, one . . .'

Susie looked. 'Who? Did he give a name?'

Harry nodded. 'Yeah, but it's no good. We can't bring him in for questioning.'

'Why not?' demanded Susie.

'Because he's dead. It's your husband – it was Mike Hazard.'

Susie turned away. Jellings called Harry over. It was now more vital than ever that Stella Hazard find their man – if he was there. Jellings looked at the screens again. 'I hope to Christ he is. Try and explain this cock-up of expenses if she can't find him! Two hundred-odd quid for a bloody hat!' He returned to his conversation with DI Stanley at Coomes, ordering him to put the pressure on Jenkins to get as much information out of him as possible.

Stella had been up at the rails, back at the bookies' stands, up at the rails again, back to the paddock area. She was rapidly getting exhausted.

'I need to go to the ladies. Will you ask them if it's all right?'

Back in the surveillance van, Jellings covered his face with his hands. 'Now she wants to go to the toilet! Can you get over to the stands afterwards, Stokes? Up in the stands, then over by the private boxes.'

Stella came out of the ladies. Stokes turned as Stella missed her footing again. 'They want us over at the stands, Mrs Hazard.'

'Right. The stands it is, then.'

She dragged her heel out of the grass, leaning against poor Stokes – as Alexander Reed passed within six feet of her.

'That's him. You see him? He's got the same tie on, different coat, but *that's him*!'

Reed was making his way towards the private boxes. Millbank had been ranting at him: no Hazard, no Kenny Graham. He was getting the wind up: something was wrong, and he reckoned they should pull out. Reed disappeared into the crowd as the news was relayed that Stella had ID'd their man.

A cheer went up from all the officers in the surveillance truck. They had Reed now, and a good description of him. They picked him up on camera after camera as he made his way through the crowds towards the private boxes. Jellings yelled for quiet. 'Any of the locals give us a name for him yet?'

As yet no one was close enough, but two men were swiftly making their way after Reed and the private boxes to get a closer look.

Stella and Stokes were now, as instructed, heading for the stands.

In the surveillance truck, Susie kept her eyes on Stella. 'Maybe as she has identified him now we should call her?'

They had lost sight of Reed. He seemed to have vanished. Details of the third race were now being announced as the horses cantered up the course to the starting post.

Reed entered Millbank's private box, where his guests were drinking champagne. He squeezed past out onto the balcony just as he heard Millbank making a call, as they had previously arranged, to his bookies. He was joking as he gave his private account number, then he let out a roar of laughter. 'Yes, I am desperate! But make my day – OK twenty, yes twenty Gs – Julianna!'

Millbank clicked off his portable, and turned to Reed. 'Where the hell have you been? They're almost under starter's orders.'

Reed was sweating. It was too late to pull out now, Millbank had started the ball rolling, and he watched as two more guests called their private account numbers in and placed identical bets – all on Julianna, all on Millbank's horse.

Reed trained his binoculars on the horses lining up for the start. He saw her, walking past the rails . . . He had to stare hard, but he was sure the woman was Stella Hazard. No Mike Hazard – but now his wife appears. Stella. So much for bloody Kenny. Reed caught his breath. The black wife, he'd said he'd seen her, the ex-cop! Reed lowered the binoculars. This was Stella Hazard – Stella, the wife Reed had got the disk from. Had she tipped off the police? No Mike, no Kenny. Reed moved off fast.

Wee Georgie, having saddled up Julianna, watched her pass through the enclosure and head down the track. He wove in and out of the jostling crowds towards a bookie. He was after placing a bet himself: he knew better than anyone just how good a horse Julianna was. She'd walk this one.

The cameras scanned slowly over the private boxes as the guests and members gathered on their balconies. They got a shot of Reed again, and this time one of the local officers was able to give his name. He was Alexander Reed, trainer for Rodney Millbank's stud. Within seconds it was known that Millbank owned the three-year-old, Julianna, running in the race, which by this time was under starter's orders. At the same time, another call came in from Coomes main betting shop: after further questioning, Colin Jenkins had come up with Reed's name.

The word went out like lightning to the bookies on the course, as the stewards made their way to the finishing line, knowing they were too late to scratch Julianna. But all the bookies were warned off taking any further bets on her; the race was being monitored by the stewards. Georgie waited, wafting his money to attract the attention of the bookie who was speaking into a portable phone. When he tried to place a bet, he was told that there was going to be a stewards' enquiry. No more bets were being taken. No more bets on Julianna.

The starting pistol cracked, and they were off . . . So was Georgie, going as fast as his short legs could carry him, running like hell to Millbank's box. He had to push and shove his way through the throng as the race was on, and by the time he got to Millbank's box, the horses were thundering past – Julianna way out in the lead. Millbank was red in the face, cheering her on. Georgie got to Reed and grabbed him.

'They're on to something'! The stewards are lined up waitin' at the finishing post. They stopped takin' bets on the course.'

Reed turned the binoculars and, sure enough, there were the stewards. He looked towards Millbank as he roared and yelled for Julianna, still way out in the lead.

Reed and Georgie made a run for it, missing the arrival of the police by seconds. They made their way back to the horse trailers. At the same time Stokes was being given the order to bring Mrs Hazard back to the truck. He could not hear clearly and stepped aside as the crowds merged around him, listening intently.

Reed came face to face with Stella – who was so shocked she stepped back. Georgie pushed her, hard: 'Keep walking, Mrs Hazard, you are going to be our ticket out. *Move!*'

Stokes was on camera, turning this way and that in confusion. 'I've lost her! I've lost her!'

They were all staring at the various screens. One moment Stella had been clearly visible, the next – Susie scanned the pictures, then ran out. Harry looked after her.

'How could they bloody lose her – *in that fuckin' hat?*'

Wee Georgie pushed Stella into the back of the horse trailer. She was gagged, the microphone ripped from her blouse. She had her feet tied up and her hands roped behind her. Reed was struggling, pushing and shoving Roman up the ramp, but the horse was acting up, eyes rolling.

'It's her hat, Gov'! For chrissakes, get her hat off – it's making him go crazy!'

Reed snatched off Stella's hat, and Roman was gradually pushed and cajoled into the horse box.

'Shut the gates, Georgie! *Hurry! Get the hell out of here!*'

Susie ran this way and that, uncertain where to start searching. Then she decided to run back to the last place they had seen Stella. She was out of breath as she looked around the members' enclosure, then she caught sight of the trucks and horse boxes lined up in the private car park beyond it.

Susie ran past two stable girls who were leading Julianna back. 'What the hell is Georgie doing? He's taking Roman out. *Eh! Georgie!*'

Susie stopped, watched the big trailer disappearing in the opposite direction. It joined two more trailers and horse boxes driving out.

'Is that horse trailer anything to do with Millbank?'

The stable girl looked at Susie. 'You got permission to be in this area? It's private. Where's your pass?'

Susie shouted, 'Is that Millbank?'

The girl nodded. Taking a deep breath, Susie took off and ran the almost half mile to the exit gates. Heaving for breath, she saw to her relief the patrol cars at the gates – but they were allowing the horse boxes out!

Susie kept on running until she was in hailing distance of one officer. 'Don't let the horse boxes out! The third one – stop it!' She struggled for breath. 'Stop the third horse box! It's Millbank's!'

Stella was curled up, terrified, as Roman kicked and swung his head from side to side. Reed inched round, attempting to quieten him but Roman swung his head up, clipping Reed's shoulder, snapping his reins. Reed stumbled. At the same time Stella began kicking hard at her partition in the next stall, in the hope that someone outside would hear her.

A patrol car, siren blasting, joined the group of police at

175

the gates. Suddenly, the combination of Stella's kicking and the sound of the police siren made Roman rear up, thrashing the air with his front hoofs, smashing one into Reed's face. Reed buckled forward, Roman, loose in the box, freaked even more, and he trampled and kicked, trampled and kicked. Reed was trapped between and beneath the powerful horse's legs.

Harry Green ran from the patrol car, Susie was yelling at the top of her lungs.

'Don't let it out! It's Millbank!'

She saw Harry – he was right in front of the trailer. Georgie was about to run him over. 'Open up the back!'

Georgie refused, said the horse was crazed, sick, there was no way he could open up. Harry reached up and dragged Georgie down from the driving seat. 'Open up!'

Georgie hadn't been kidding when he said the horse was crazed. Roman was now frothing at the mouth, and as Georgie unlocked the back doors his hind legs kicked up, Roman backed out wildly and bolted.

Stella was safe. Scared, but safe – and Susie had never been so relieved to see anyone in her life. She hugged Stella, held her so tightly she almost winded her. She was crying, 'You're OK! Oh, God, I was so scared, Stella – Stella, I was so scared!'

Stella was still gagged, her eyes popping out of her head. Susie removed the gag, and Stella leaned against her. Bits of her new hat were scattered around the horse box. 'Dear God, I hope they won't make me pay for that hat. Will you look what the horse has done to it!'

Roman had kicked Reed to death. The body was covered as Stella was helped out and into a patrol car. Susie remained with her as they took her statement.

It was early evening by the time they both got home, the baby having been collected from Mrs Donald. Susie watched Stella serving fish and chips from the paper. Plates heating in the oven, tomato ketchup at the ready, bread and butter cut . . .

They sat down, Stella remarking that it was a bit of a come-down after the five star hotel. Then she produced two bottles of Guinness, saying it would keep Susie fit. She poured two glasses. Susie sensed that something was going on – there was a glint to Stella.

'I have a proposition to make. It's about the agency, about Seekers.'

Susie picked up the Guinness, then put it down again. 'You see that holdall on the sideboard? Well, open it, go on, open it!' Stella urged.

Susie got up and unzipped the holdall. 'Where did you get this from?'

Stella sipped the Guinness, then opened the ketchup. 'Mike. Now just sit down and stay calm. He came to the hotel! He threatened me, but I went right back at him. I told him that we wanted to be left alone. Now, was that the right thing or not?'

Susie picked up her glass again. 'Go on.'

'I made him promise, swear to me, that he would never come back. In return, we would not report him to the police. I wouldn't get arrested and he could go to wherever the hell he liked, so long as he left us to get on with our lives. Now that is what I told him, and I took this – there's almost thirteen thousand quid in there, Susie, and I'm going to split it right down the middle.'

Susie gulped at the Guinness. 'You mean it?'

'Yes, I do. I'll just have to have a drink, I'm parched.' Stella took a few sips, carefully putting the glass down. She jabbed at her fish and chips. 'But there is a condition. I want to open up Seekers, we've enough money, and—'

Susie shot to her feet. 'Wait! Wait – you mean I can run the agency? You're letting me have the agency? Yes?'

Stella nodded. 'Yes. We'll both run it!'

Susie laughed. 'What?'

'I said, we'll both run it. We'll be sort of – partners!'

'What? Oh, I get it. You mean you'll be like a sleeping partner? Is that what you mean? OK, I can go along with that.'

Stella drained her glass and banged it down. 'No! *I don't mean sleeping.* I've been doing that for most of my life. Now, well, I want to be a part of it.'

Susie was deflated. 'Partner. But, Stella, you don't know anything about being on an investigation.'

'So I can learn. I'll pick it up!'

Susie shook salt over her chips. Then she picked up her knife and fork.

'Well, what do you say? Susie?'

Susie chewed a big mouthful. 'I'm thinking about it. Do I pay you rent? Do you still want me living here with the baby?'

Stella nodded. Susie helped herself to some ketchup. It could work she thought, if she was running the office, she was going to need someone to look after Mike. It could work . . .

'Yeah. OK. We'll have a go – we've nothing to lose. Yes! We'll open the business!'

Stella beamed. She put out her hand. 'Shake – partner!'

Susie winced slightly, but she clasped Stella's hand. 'Partner.'

Stella slept soundly for the first night in months. She had dreams of buying a cottage like the woman detective in *Murder She Wrote*, the TV series she watched avidly. She'd get some half-moon glasses, smart suits, go on a diet. Maybe even take some self-defence classes, or she could go to a shooting gallery, learn how to handle a gun. Everything seemed possible, her life was opening up – it was exciting. She might be menopausal, but she was not as broke as she had first thought, nor as empty inside, and when she got cracking on that office, a bit of paint here and there . . . She had drifted into a deep sleep thinking about what colour blinds she should or shouldn't suggest to Susie.

Susie was restless, chewing everything over. Would it work? Could she make it work? She reckoned if she got Stella under control, devised a strict work-to-rule regime, it would be possible . . . If the baby became Stella's priority, then that would leave more time for Susie to get the office set up and rolling.

She reckoned they would just have enough to keep it open, but it was going to be hard. Suddenly she thought of Sherry. Would it be a good idea to have Sherry come to work for them? A whizz-kid on the computers, she'd be cheap, act as a trainee, she could train her, and Stella could stay on at home as chef, bottle-washer and baby-minder. She would make it work – she knew she could! Suddenly the future looked good, she felt good. Just like Stella, for the first time in ages she had forgotten about Mike. The future was opening up for her. Susie curled up tightly, like a kid. She was looking forward to it, she was happy!

Mike Hazard eased open the office door. He had intended to kip down in the boat but discovered a comatose Al Franks in his ex-army sleeping bag occupying the cabin.

Mike washed and brewed a cup of tea as he made plans for the future. He wanted to make it up with Susie, and obviously to see his son. He wanted a future. Right now there wasn't one, but he would survive, he always had.

As Mike finished his tea, he caught a glimpse of himself in the kitchen mirror. He seemed to stare into a stranger's face. It was an eerie feeling, and he turned out the lights, almost as if he did not want to see what he had become. Maybe, he told himself, he should do as Stella had asked. Maybe he should go away and never come back. He had promised never to see them again, promised on his son's life. The boy he had always wanted, and yet had never even held in his arms.

Mike Hazard walked silently over the canal bridge, a man of broken dreams and broken promises. He wouldn't make any moves yet, he needed time to heal his wounds. He needed time to heal, and then, then he would come back.

SEEKERS 2

Stella and Susie form a partnership to run the Seekers Investigation Agency. They are an ill-matched pair, and nothing is ever easy, but their friendship deepens. They hire Sherry Donald as a secretary, presuming her to be a computer genius, but not until Sherry is asked to type a letter do they realize she is illiterate.

The mystery and secrets surrounding their husband, Mike Hazard, continue. He needs money, he wants his son, but he cannot make up his mind which wife to settle for.

Ex-police woman Susie attempts to train Stella in detection, but their first case requires Stella's immediate participation. She is hired to discover which member of an over-forties dating agency is an adept burglar! At the same time Susie starts work on their second assignment, providing evidence for a divorce case.

Business is looking reasonable if not good, but then what began as a simple open-and-shut investigation of a husband's infidelities, spirals into a terrifying murder hunt.

LYNDA LA PLANTE

ENTWINED

£4.99

THE BRILLIANT NEW NOVEL
FROM LYNDA LA PLANTE

In the newly liberated streets of modern Berlin two
women, a pampered, beautiful Baroness, losing control of
her mind, and a fearless wild animal trainer, facing the
greatest challenge of her career, are drawn together by a
series of tragic and extraordinary coincidences.

When a man is found brutally murdered, their lives become
entangled by an investigation that uncovers a web of
darkness and opens up secrets that have long been
condemned to silence . . .

Who were they, all those years ago? What nightmares did
they share? And what is the truth about the undying nature
of their love?

LYNDA LA PLANTE

THE LEGACY

£5.99

'A saga to end all sagas . . .'
SUNDAY EXPRESS

1905 – 1945
The Legacy was a curse . . .

For Hugh – the hard-drinking, two-fisted lion of the Welsh valleys. For his loyal daughter Evelyne – who lost her heart and her father's trust to the charm of a travelling gypsy. And for handsome prizefighter Freedom – saved from the gallows to do battle for the heavyweight championship of the world . . .

From the poverty of the Welsh pit valleys to the glories of the prize ring, from the dangers of Prohibition America to the terrors of Britain at war, Lynda La Plante begins the bestselling saga of their lives and their fortunes . . . and the curse that made their name . . .

This Pan edition contains Books 1-5 of *The Legacy*, first published in hardback by Sidgwick & Jackson. Books 6-14 of *The Legacy* appear in *The Talisman*, also available in Pan Books.

LYNDA LA PLANTE

THE TALISMAN

£5.99

'. . . *a blockbuster of a novel*'
SUNDAY EXPRESS

1945 – 1980

The Talisman is the key to a fortune . . .

For Edward – the brilliant scholar who inherited his father's looks . . . and his father's curse. For Alex, his brother, whose quest for revenge fuelled an empire built on corruption. And for Evelyne and Juliana, the fourth generation, still haunted by the secrets of their family's past.

From the gold mines of South Africa to the boardrooms of the City of London, from the risks of the casinos to the heady glamour of the London fashion, Lynda La Plante continues the bestselling saga of a family's lives and fortunes . . . and the curse that made their name . . .

'*A torrid tale of love, intrigue, and passion . . . packed with glamour and set against the London world of big business and big, big money*'
DAILY EXPRESS

This Pan edition contains Books 6-14 of *The Legacy*, first published in hardback by Sidgwick & Jackson. Books 1-5 are published as *The Legacy* in Pan Books.

LYNDA LA PLANTE

PRIME SUSPECT

£3.99

She fought for the right to lead a murder enquiry, they fought for the chance to stop her . . .

Detective Chief Inspector Jane Tennison came through the ranks the hard way, opposed and resented at every step. Then she inherited a murder enquiry – and the boys lined up to watch her fall.

Tennison needed proof. Anything she could find to make the charges stick.

And that was when she turned up the second body . . .

All Pan books are available at your local bookshop or newsagent, or can be ordered direct from the publisher. Indicate the number of copies required and fill in the form below.

Send to: Pan C. S. Dept
             Macmillan Distribution Ltd
             Houndmills Basingstoke RG21 2XS
or phone: 0256 29242, quoting title, author and Credit Card number.

Please enclose a remittance* to the value of the cover price plus: £1.00 for the first book plus 50p per copy for each additional book ordered.

*Payment may be made in sterling by UK personal cheque, postal order, sterling draft or international money order, made payable to Pan Books Ltd.

Alternatively by Barclaycard/Access/Amex/Diners

Card No. | | | | | | | | | | | | | | | | | | |

Expiry Date | | | | | |

_____

Signature:

Applicable only in the UK and BFPO addresses

While every effort is made to keep prices low, it is sometimes necessary to increase prices at short notice. Pan Books reserve the right to show on covers and charge new retail prices which may differ from those advertised in the text or elsewhere.

NAME AND ADDRESS IN BLOCK LETTERS PLEASE:

....

Name _____

Address _____

_____

_____

_____

6/92